SWEET SUNRISE

Kay Correll

First Printing, 2017

052417

Published by ROSE QUARTZ PRESS

ISBN-13: 978-1-944761-00-4

INDIGO BAY SWEET ROMANCE SERIES

Read all the books in this multi-author sweet romance series set in South Carolina. The books can be read in any order so jump in with any book!

Sweet Dreams - Stacy Claflin

Sweet Matchmaker - Jean Oram

Sweet Sunrise - Kay Correll

Sweet Illusions - Jeanette Lewis

Sweet Regrets - Jennifer Peel

Sweet Rendezvous - Danielle Stewart

Chapter One

The last place on earth Will Layton thought he'd ever be was back in Indigo Bay, South Carolina. He'd dusted the sand off from the town years ago and sworn he'd never grace its small-town streets again.

But here he was.

And the one and only person in the whole wide world who could make him come back here was his younger sister. Whitney said she needed him, so here he was, driving down Main Street.

The town looked the same, though some of the businesses had changed names since he'd last visited.

In spite of his good intentions, he couldn't help himself, he turned off Main Street, cut across a side street, and headed to the area of Indigo Bay where they'd lived until his sister left for college. He turned down a narrow street crowded with small homes and apartments. There it was. His childhood home, more bedraggled than it had been when he'd grown up in it, if that was possible.

He slowed down and rolled past the apartment. He could still picture himself racing out the front door, clattering down the stairs, hurrying to school or one of his many jobs. He stepped on the accelerator and pulled away from the apartment building and the memories.

He glanced at the address he'd written on the back of a bar tab from The Lucky Duck, a tavern he owned on Belle Island, Florida. His little sister sure had come up in the world to be able to afford to live on Seaside Boulevard.

Will crossed over to Seaside, with its rows of beach cottages mixed in with large, elaborate homes lining the coast. It was just a short distance from where he'd grown up, but it seemed like the other side of the world.

He carefully searched the addresses until he came to 1203 Seaside Boulevard. A pretty, mint-green cottage with white trim graced the lot. He pulled onto the sand and crushed-shell driveway and took a deep breath. He could do this.

He could.

Probably.

He climbed out of his truck and stretched. It had been a long drive from Belle Island to Indigo Bay and he'd only stopped once, briefly, then sped on to his two week sentence, as he'd begun to think of this trip. The sooner he got here, the sooner he could leave. Well, that wasn't exactly right. He'd promised his sister he'd stay two weeks. Fourteen days. Three hundred thirty-six hours. But who's counting?

The front door flew open and Whitney came bounding down the stairs and threw herself into his arms.

"Willie. You did come. I wasn't sure."

He grinned and swept his petite sister off her feet. "I said I would. Have I ever lied to you?"

"Probably." She grinned back at him. "Is that all you brought?" She eyed his one small duffle.

He figured if he packed light it would be easier to escape…

"I need to tell you something before we go inside." Whitney shifted away from him, tugging at a lock of her short blonde pixie cut.

He knew that look… He stared at her suspiciously. "What?"

"I… um… well, Dad is here. He got released from a rehab place this morning and I decided to bring him to my house instead of bringing him back to his apartment. He needs someone to help him while he recovers. I just… want to take care of him."

Will barely kept from flinching at the sucker punch his sister just threw him. "So he's trying to quit drinking again? You talked him into rehab?"

"No, it's not that. He's been injured in an accident."

"Hope he didn't hurt anyone else."

3

"Willie, no, listen to me—"

Will held up a hand. "I don't want to hear it. I thought when you said you were overwhelmed with life, you needed help with your *jewelry business*. You said you were getting audited and needed help." Will's heart pounded in his chest. He wasn't ready for this.

Not yet. Not now. Probably not ever.

He needed time to adjust to the fact he was even back in Indigo Bay.

"I *am* overwhelmed and I do need help with my business, you've always been a whiz with numbers. And I *do* need help taking care of Dad for a while." Her blue eyes clouded. "Please, Willie. Don't be difficult. He's changed." His sister tugged on his hand. "Come in. You'll see."

"Whit, I love you. I do. But I am *not* staying under the same roof as that man. I promised myself years ago."

Whitney threw him her best pleading look. The one he could never resist, whether it was asking him for pizza money or help with her homework when they were kids… or evidently when she asked him to see their father, now that they were adults. She was the one person in the world he'd do anything for.

Almost anything.

She tugged on his hand one more time. "Please?"

He sighed and picked up his duffle. "Okay, I'm coming."

He trailed behind his sister and slowly climbed the

stairs to her front door. A door that was surely leading to a path he wasn't ready to take.

* * * * *

Dr. Ashley Harden closed the door to the clinic and flipped the sign to "closed." She leaned against the back of the door, exhausted. It had been a long day with a constant stream of patients and a handful of emergencies. She'd been more than eager to take over Doc Browning's practice while he took a leave of absence due to his wife's health. She was hoping he'd keep her on when he came back if she could grow the practice for him. Today she could have used a second pair of hands, but it was just she and the front desk worker, Jerri Lynn.

She shoved off the door and slipped out of her lab coat. The coat was tastefully embroidered with "Dr. Harden." It still startled her a bit when people called her that. It had been a long, hard road to get to this point.

She walked through the clinic checking on things and turning off lights. She'd sent Jerri Lynn home an hour or so ago and had seen the last few patients on her own. Unlike Ashley, Jerri Lynn had a family to get home to each night.

She walked out the back door to the clinic and locked it behind her. The warm evening air drifted down the street, and she reached up to free the braid that held her long, auburn hair. It tumbled around her shoulders, and she shook her head to let the last strands escape. That felt better. The simple act of unleashing her hair let her transform from professional doctor Ashley to just plain Ashley.

She cut down a cross street and headed down Seaside Boulevard to the cottage she was renting on the beach. She slipped off her shoes and crossed the beach to the shoreline. The sand was warm and welcoming on her bare feet. It had become her nightly ritual to walk along the beach and unwind on her way home.

She'd considered buying her own home, but never seemed to make time in her schedule to actually look for a place. Maybe if she took the time and found her own home, she'd feel more like she belonged here, and less like an imposter. Of course, she didn't even know if she'd have a job after Doc Browning returned.

Ashley sighed. There were times when she felt like she was a little girl playing make believe she was a doctor.

* * * * *

Will stood on the deck at Whitney's cottage. So far he'd been lucky and avoided his father, who'd been sound asleep in a guest room. Evading his father for as long as possible suited Will just fine. He scrubbed a hand across his face, feeling the scruff of a day's worth of whiskers. He wanted to high-tail it back to Belle Island, but he'd never been a coward. Maybe it was time to face his demons and see his father again.

A lone woman walked towards him on the beach, slowly meandering up the shoreline at the water's edge. She reminded him a lot of Ashley, his first love—heck his only one—a woman he'd also done his best to push from all conscious thought.

His father *and* Ashely were both off-limits as far as he was concerned. He'd promised himself he would waste no time thinking about them and the what-ifs of his past.

The woman came closer and started up the beach toward the row of cottages. He froze as she got close enough for him to see every little detail, the reddish-brown hair falling around her shoulders, the long slender legs, he even remembered the way she walked. He gripped the railing of the deck and his breath caught in his throat.

The woman looked up and saw him. She came to an abrupt stop.

They both stood suspended in time, looking at each other, shocked to be thrown together again. She finally took the last few strides to the bottom of the stairs and looked up at him. "Will."

"Ashley." He searched her face, noting the changes. She'd lost the young high school girl look, replaced with a more serious and mature presence. Her emerald-green eyes looked at him expectantly. He fought the urge to either take the few steps down to her or turn and run. "What are you doing here, Ashley?"

"I could ask the same thing."

"I'm here visiting my sister." He noticed his knuckles had gone white from gripping the railing so tightly, and he forced himself to release his hold.

"She didn't mention you were coming." Her voice sounded exactly the same—deep, throaty and... enchanting.

No, it didn't.

He was no longer under that spell.

He cleared his throat. "Strange. She failed to mention you were back here, either." He could hear the cold edge to his voice. His mind reeled. What else had his sister conveniently forgotten to tell him?

"You're here to help with your father?"

"You know about him?"

She paused, one graceful hand resting on the stair rail. "I'm... I'm his doctor."

Doctor. Ashley was a doctor now. She'd made it. Done what she said she'd do all those years ago. But of course she had. He really hadn't doubted it. When Ashley set her mind on something, she never wavered, not for a moment.

"Another fact Whit forgot to mention." The air around him was devoid of oxygen, and he sucked in a couple of deep breaths, trying to get his focus, trying to steady his safe little world that had just come crashing down around him.

"I'm renting the cottage next door." Ashley nodded in the direction of the neighboring building. The cottage that was way too close to Whitney's, as far as he was concerned. He'd prefer Ashley live on the other side of the world, but if she had to live in Indigo Bay, couldn't she have at least picked a place on the other side of town?

"Oh." He didn't know what else to say. His mind was scrambled with thoughts and memories and frustrations.

And he wanted to strangle his sister.

Chapter Two

Ashley stood staring at Will. He looked good. Really good. His boyish frame had filled out to a more mature body. His brown hair was in need of a trim, as usual. The shadow of whiskers now covered the angles of his face. His chestnut brown eyes flashed with anger, or maybe it was uncertainty. So many memories swirled around her. She hadn't been prepared to see Will again, and she didn't like surprises. Not at all. She planned her life out, and didn't like to be caught off-guard.

She knew she should say something like "It's good to see you…" but she was pretty sure it *wasn't* good to see Will. She didn't need any complications now, she was focused on her practice. She'd made tough decisions in the past regarding Will, and she didn't want to relive them now.

"I… " She shifted back and took her hand off the railing. "How long are you here?"

"Two weeks." His eyes never left her face.

Two weeks might as well be two years, or twenty. She was never going to survive two weeks of Will in Indigo Bay. He'd always been her Achilles heel, her weakness.

She straightened her shoulders, determined to overcome this minor—*major*—complication in her life. "Well, I guess I'll be seeing you around, then." She deliberately made her voice sound nonchalant.

His piercing look scanned her face as she tried desperately to appear unaffected by seeing him, by his intense gaze, by the way the mature version of Will looked... well, he looked tantalizing in a dangerous way.

"I guess you will." His voice was low, almost a growl of warning.

"I'm pretty busy at work, though. I'm not here at the cottage much. I do have to check on your dad some, though. But I'm not here much." She'd already said that. She was blathering now. "I should go."

He nodded and said not a word.

* * * * *

"Whitney." Will called out her name as he slammed into the cottage. "Where are you?"

His sister came into the room. "Shhh. Dad's still asleep. Keep your voice down."

"Are there any more surprises you have planned for me? Any other secrets you've been keeping?"

"What are you talking about?"

"Oh, little details like Ashley lives next door?" He

pinned her with a glare.

She had the decency to blush. "I didn't think you'd come home if you knew she was back."

"I wouldn't have, and by the way, this is *not* home. Not for me."

Whitney crossed the room and rested a hand on his arm. "Ashley and I have actually become friends since she's been back. It's nice to have a friend right next door, someone to talk to."

"How great for you," he said without a trace of sincerity.

"Don't be like that. She's a really great person. I know you two broke up, but that was years and years ago. You were kids."

And yet it seemed like just yesterday and the pain always hovered right below the surface. You'd think he'd be over it by now, but no. He never let himself really dwell on it, except for, you know, when she showed up on the steps to the deck where he was standing.

"Whit, you've blindsided me twice today."

"I didn't mean to. I just... well, I wish you'd give Dad a chance. And I should have told you about Ashley, I should have. I'm sorry." She used that same he-couldn't-say-no-to, pleading look with him.

He let out a long whoosh of air and raked his hands through his hair. He did want to strangle his little sister, but then he could tell she was overwhelmed. She looked tired and stressed. He would help because that's what he always did, no matter what. It was always Whitney before Will as far as he was concerned.

"Whitney?"

Will froze at the sound of his father's voice. A voice that haunted him, taunted him, mocked his dreams.

His father rolled into the room in a wheelchair.

"Dad, I would have helped you get into the chair." Whitney rushed over to their father.

"You're doing enough for me as it is. I can manage."

His father looked up and saw him standing next to Whitney. Will locked eyes with the man for the first time in almost ten years.

"Son." His father looked at Will cautiously.

"Warren." He would not give the man the satisfaction of being called Dad.

"How have you been?"

"Just great. Perfect. Couldn't be better." Except for all of the surprises being hurled at him today.

"Whitney said she asked you to come. I didn't think you would."

"If I'd known you were going to be here, I wouldn't." *How's that for honesty?*

"Don't be like that, Willie." Whitney rested her hand on her father's shoulder.

Warren reached up and covered Whitney's hand with his own. Will wanted to stride over there and rip the man's hand away. He had no right, none at all, to be acting all fatherly with Whit.

"It's okay." His father intervened. "I deserve that. And more."

Will remained silent.

"I know I can't make it up to you. I wasn't there for you. For either of you. I'm so very sorry. I've changed, though."

"Heard it before, Warren." Will didn't buy it. It was all just words with his father. Broken promises. A roller-coaster ride of attempts to get sober, then back in the bottle with the drunken ugliness that accompanied it. Rinse and repeat.

His father looked up at Whitney. "I should go back to my own place. I'll be fine."

"No, you won't. You need help while you get stronger." Whitney turned to Will, her eyes flashing. "Quit being such a jerk."

He had to escape, get out, regain his balance. "I'm going to go get something to eat."

"I made dinner."

He was not going to sit down at a dinner table like they were some kind of family. A family that included Warren.

"I'll be back later." Way later. When he was sure Warren was sound asleep.

Whitney sent him a look that told him exactly what she thought of him right now. But he didn't care. He had to escape the fantasy family dinner Whitney was trying to inflict on him. Not that they were a *family*.

15

"Tomorrow we'll go to your shop and I'll look at your books. But as far as Warren goes, he's not my problem." Will spun on his heels and banged his way out of the cottage, letting the screen door slam behind him.

He probably *was* being a jerk, but he couldn't stop himself.

* * * * *

Will drove aimlessly down the streets of Indigo Bay. He had no plan and nowhere to go really— except away from Whitney's cottage. Her cottage where his father was staying. Her cottage where Ashley lived right next door. He was reasonably certain he hated her cute little cottage right now.

He pulled into a parking spot on Main Street and slid out of the car. He looked to the left, then the right, then back to the left.

He was trapped in a time warp of memories and reality, of being a kid in Indigo Bay, and being an adult back for a visit. A visit that wasn't exactly turning out how he planned.

The welcoming sign of Sweet Caroline's caught his attention, and he turned that direction. He had no clue if Caroline still ran the place, but at least it seemed like an oasis in the desert of the day he was having.

He tugged opened the door to the restaurant, and the familiar scents reached out and wrapped around him. The hint of cinnamon goodness from her sweet rolls, the fried food, the aroma of the best coffee Indigo Bay had to offer, all wrapped up in a welcoming package of good memories. Just about the only decent memories he had of the town. He looked around the place and saw it hadn't changed, which suited him just fine. He didn't need any more surprises today.

"Will Layton, you come over here." Caroline came out from behind the counter and rushed up to him. She wrapped him in a comforting hug, then stepped back, a hand on each of his shoulders. "You look good, Will."

"You look fabulous, as ever. Getting younger looking every day." Will winked.

"Always were a sweet talker." Caroline grinned. "What brings you to Indigo Bay?"

"Whitney called and said she needed help."

"Oh, with your father? I heard he was laid up in an accident."

How could he have forgotten the almost scary way everyone knew everyone else's business in town? Though, to be honest, it wasn't much different in his own town of Belle Island. "Well, the dad thing came as a bit of a shock to me."

Caroline eyed him for a moment, then nodded. "I suspected as much."

Caroline knew him so well. He'd worked at Sweet Caroline's from the day he'd been old enough to hold down a job, to the day he left town, along with any other job he could get his hands on. Anything to provide for his sister when his father hit rock bottom again and again. Caroline probably had suspected some of the truth about their home situation, even though Will had worked diligently to hide their reality from the prying eyes of the town, and hoped it was the one secret the town would never learn. His father would disappear for days at a time, and Will worked hard to earn enough to put food on the table and take care of his sister, always wondering if Warren would actually show up again. The man eventually did return with an apology and a promise that it wouldn't happen again.

Until it did.

Caroline had let Whitney sit at a table and do her homework while Will worked, so his sister wouldn't have to be home alone. She often gave both of them their meals for the day. Caroline knew his father was a drinker, but Will had always hidden the detail that he also disappeared for days at a time. He'd always been afraid some social worker would come and take Whitney away.

Will stood and looked at the woman who had so influenced his life and helped him survive in those very hard days. Her welcoming hug soothed his jangled nerves, and the familiar atmosphere of Sweet Caroline's allowed him finally to feel like he could breathe.

"I expect you're starving." Caroline smiled at him.

"Always."

"Come take a seat and have dinner. It's on the house."

"Thanks." Will slid into a chair in a corner table, out of the way, hoping to avoid seeing anyone else he knew.

Later Caroline brought him his meal and sat across from him, chatting and telling him things that had changed in the town. There was a new gazebo at the public beach area. A fancy clothing store had opened, along with a new bookstore.

"My son, Dallas, bought the Indigo Bay Cottages—you remember them—and runs them now. He seems very happy ." Caroline's eyes shone when she talked of her son.

"That's great." Not that he'd know what it was like to live in the same town as family.

Caroline bounced on to another subject. "You know, Will, your sister is really overwhelmed right now. I can tell. She was in here yesterday for a quick bite to eat. She looked tired."

"I know she is." And he felt guilty about it, he did. But he did not want to deal with his father. Maybe Whit had been tricked into forgiving him, but Will wasn't at that point. He might never be. But then, he had given up more than Whit had back then.

"Well, you might want to cut her some slack. I know you have your differences with your father, but I think Whitney has made her peace with him. You should give her that. We all deal with our past in our own way."

Caroline always had been the one to speak her mind and give advice. He simply wasn't sure he was ready to take guidance from anyone right now, so he merely nodded.

Caroline stood. "Well, think about it anyway, and I'm always here if you need to talk."

Will watched her walk away to wait on another customer and suddenly felt so very alone. He glanced at his watch. He had hours and hours to kill before it was safe to go back to Whit's.

Chapter Three

Ashley padded around the cottage getting ready for work. She usually took her coffee out to the deck to watch the sunrise, but she was afraid she'd see Will. He was also an early-morning person. Or at least he used to be. Who knew what he was like now? But anyway, she wasn't going to chance it. She wasn't ready for another run-in with Will.

She'd been shocked to see him standing on Whitney's deck last night. She was surprised Whitney hadn't told her Will was coming, but then she hadn't seen Whitney in days. The clinic had been ridiculously busy with a virus that seemed to be spreading its misery indiscriminately through the town.

Ashley had such conflicted feelings when it came to Will. He'd been her first love, probably only love. She'd dated some in college and med school, but mostly she'd stuck to the books to make sure her grades stayed high and she kept her scholarships. Even then, she'd graduated with a load of debt to pay off, more than she'd planned. She hated it when her carefully planned life took a detour.

Will, though, he always took detours with gusto. She'd never seen him plan a thing. She didn't understand how a person could have no big goals in life. He just made snap decisions and went with them. He'd even dropped out of high school. That had been the last straw in their relationship. She couldn't go out with a person who just wanted to wander through life. They were just too different.

She rinsed her mug and set it in the dishwasher. She looked around the room to make sure everything was picked up before she left. She liked everything to be in place, nice and neat when she came home from work. She straightened a stack of magazines she hadn't found time to read yet—and the stack kept growing larger and larger. She'd get around to reading them soon, she was sure of it. She'd picked up home decorating magazines and health magazines. She'd even picked up a knitting magazine, because she'd always wanted to learn to knit. That would happen right after she found the time to read the magazines…

She left by the front door and decided to walk down the street to the clinic today. Will had been a beach walker and she didn't want to run into him on the beach. Or anywhere. She let out an impatient huff of breath.

Will was back in town and already she was changing her carefully laid out routine.

She took off at a brisk pace, wanting to get to work early and look through some charts before the day started. The early morning sun warmed her skin, and she plucked her sunglasses from atop her head and settled them on her face. It was going to be one of those perfect days in Indigo Bay.

Except for the fact that Will was staying right next door to her cottage.

* * * * *

Will had gotten up before dawn and slipped out of Whitney's cottage. He'd left a note saying he'd meet her at her shop, Coastal Creations, at nine. He'd gone to the point to see the sunrise, then wandered around town, killing time. Tourists strolled along the streets in search of early morning coffee and breakfast. A young couple walked by, pushing a set of red-haired twins in a stroller. A trio of twenty-something girls—or would that be women—walked past him in short-shorts and tank tops, laughing in that way that good female friends have. He couldn't help himself, he turned and gave them an appreciative look as they passed. One of them turned and looked back at him and grinned. He grinned in return and continued walking down the street.

Promptly at nine he pushed through the door to Whitney's shop. His sister looked up from the counter. "There you are."

"There I am," he answered.

"You can't avoid Dad forever."

"Do you want help, or not? Because I can just hop back in my car and head back to Belle Island." He knew his voice was short-tempered, but he couldn't help it.

Whitney opened her mouth, then closed it. She then looked directly at him. "Okay, I won't push it. But I do need your help here and I could also use your help with Dad."

"Books, yes. Warren, no. Show me the books."

Whitney led the way to a back office. It was crammed with stacks of folders, pictures of her jewelry pieces on the wall, and a long table where she sat and designed her work.

"Whit, this place is a mess."

"I'm a creative. We thrive in chaos."

"Well, you really should be flourishing here, then." Will shook his head.

"Okay, it's a bit out of control. When Shawna Jacobson came to town when she was shooting that movie nearby, she bought a jewelry set from me—the whole set, mind you, necklace, bracelet and earrings— she posted on her social media account about how much she loved it. The post went viral and I got so many orders. I hired workers to help me make the jewelry and keep up. My bookwork kind of took a back seat. The movie director came in and got some more pieces and used them in the movie. Well, it's been crazy since then.

Good crazy, but crazy."

"That was more than a year ago."

"Yes, and it did make a name for me and I've been doing really well since then. But I'm in over my head with all the bookwork stuff. Now I got a letter from the IRS about an audit."

"How about hiring an accountant?" He eyed the stacks of pages.

"Two different ones. One left town and sold his business to this new guy. But he's… probably even more overwhelmed than I am. I filed my taxes… but now the IRS wants to audit my books. You can help me, right?"

Will scrubbed a hand across his face and took a seat at the desk. "I can try. Let me look through these folders and you boot up your accounting software on the computer for me."

"About that… I'm a bit behind on keeping up with my accounting."

Will tilted his head. "How behind?"

"A bit." Whitney blushed. "Okay, a lot. I told you I needed you."

Will stared at the stack of papers spread across the desk. Whit had always been the artistic one, the free spirit, the… messy one. "Okay, you go do what you do best. Sell jewelry. I'll start looking at all of this and see what I can do."

"You're my favorite brother."

"Don't you forget it." Will picked up the closest pile of

papers and started to sort through them.

* * * * *

Ashley looked at the clinic's daily schedule. A busy day, but doable. Though somehow a doable day always became an impossibly busy day with emergencies filtering in along with the scheduled patients.

The morning had stayed mostly on schedule, kind of. She glanced at the chart in her hand. Mia Tanner, seven years old. Mother, Victoria Tanner. She knocked on the door of the exam room and entered. There stood her impeccably dressed, slender bodied, perfect-hair nemesis from her high school days. She hadn't caught that Victoria Tanner would be Vicki *Holloway* Tanner.

Ashley pulled on her best doctor imitation to cover her surprise. "I didn't realize—"

Vicki looked at Ashley for a long moment, sweeping her glance from Ashley's messy braid to her practical standing-on-my-feet-all-day shoes. "Ashley."

"Hello, Vicki."

"I go by Victoria now. No one calls me Vicki." Vicki-Victoria flipped her blonde hair behind her shoulder with a graceful flick of her perfectly manicured fingers. "I usually bring Mia into Charleston, but the doctor there couldn't fit her in at any time that would work with my schedule. I decided to try the clinic here and see if you could figure out what's wrong with her."

Ashley turned to the young girl. "Hello, Mia. What seems to be wrong?"

"I—"

"Her stomach hurts, no fever, a bit of the sniffles." Vicki cut her daughter off before she could answer for herself.

"How long have you been feeling like this?" Ashley asked the girl.

Once again Vicki answered. "Two days. Long enough. I need her to get better. I have a busy weekend coming up with the Ashland Belle Society's fundraiser this weekend."

How *inconvenient* for Vicki's daughter to pick this week to get sick... Vicki hadn't changed a bit. It was still all about her.

"There's a virus going around now. Same symptoms. But let me take a look at her."

Ashley did a quick exam and decided the girl most likely had the same flu that half a dozen people had come in with today. "I could run some more tests, but I think the best thing to do would be to just let the virus run its course. If she gets worse or shows any other symptoms, of course call me or bring her back in."

"I'm sorry I got sick, Mommy." Mia's eyes filled with tears.

"It's not your fault, sweetie. Sometimes these viruses just get to you." Ashley knelt in front of the girl. "It's not something you did."

Mia nodded and swiped a tear on her face.

"So, you're not going to do anything for her? Give her

anything?" Vicki's eyes flashed in disbelief.

Ashley looked at Vicki. "An antibiotic isn't going to help this."

"So you're doing *nothing*?" Vicki stood with a hand on one hip and a look of irritation plastered across her face. "Do you think she'll be well by this weekend?"

"I'm not sure. Maybe. But she'll probably still be tired from fighting it."

"Just great." Vicki turned, grabbed Mia's hand, and opened the exam door. "I knew I should have taken the time to go into Charleston to a real doctor. This was a waste of my time. Come on, Mia." Her voice carried out into the waiting room, and quite a few of the patients looked up to see who was causing such a commotion. Jerri Lynn sent Ashley a questioning look, but Ashley just shrugged.

Vicki-Victoria stalked out of the exam room, tugging Mia along behind her. She didn't bother to stop at the reception desk and ask about a bill. She just huffed through the waiting room and slammed out the front door.

Ashley stood in the doorway to the exam room and watched her leave. Displeasing Vicki Holloway—no Victoria Tanner—was not going to help with attracting more patients and getting a good reputation here in town.

Some things never seemed to change. Vicki would always look at Ashley like she was a second-class citizen who didn't deserve to fit in with the cool crowd. Not in high school, and not now as an adult.

No, some things never did seem to change no matter how hard she worked at it.

Chapter Four

So far, Will was pretty proud of himself for avoiding his father and Ashley today. He only wished Whitney's bookwork was going as well as his avoidance plans. He sorted through the paperwork and jotted numbers on a pad of paper, along with a long list of things to investigate. It would take him every bit of the two weeks he'd promised Whit to get things straightened out for her. Not that he believed she'd still keep up with this when he left. He was going to find her a bookkeeper to hire before he left town. He added that to his growing to-do list.

A loud crash reverberated through the shop, and he jumped up from his seat. "Whit? You okay?" He hurried out into the shop. His sister sprawled on the floor, jewelry pieces and broken glass from a display case surrounded her.

"I... no. I'm not okay." Whitney held one hand in the

other, with drops of blood splattering the floor.

"Let me see it." He lowered himself carefully beside her, looked at her hand, and commanded himself to remain calm. "That's going to need stitches."

"I thought so." Whitney's face had paled to a dull ashen color.

"Don't faint on me," he warned.

"Trying not to."

Will shucked off his t-shirt and wrapped it tightly around Whitney's hand. "Let me help you up. Watch all the glass. We need to get you some help."

He carefully pulled his sister to her feet, and she leaned heavily against him.

"Can you lock up the place? The back door is unlocked, too. Keys are hanging on a hook in the office." Whit's face was a horrible shade of yellow-white and he really did fear she would pass out.

He was loath to leave her, but levered her carefully onto a chair. He grabbed the keys and locked the back door and hurried back to Whitney. "Okay, let's get you looked at."

"The only place in town right now is Ashley's clinic."

"What happened to Doc Browning?"

"He's on an extended leave. His wife is ill. Ashley's working his practice while he's gone."

Will gritted his teeth. "Okay, off to the clinic then. Same place?"

"Yes, right down the street about a block."

He helped Whitney to her feet and wrapped an arm around her waist. "Let's take your car."

"I walked to work."

"You think you can walk to the clinic?"

"I think so."

They walked out of the shop and he locked the door behind them. Whitney leaned against him as they headed down the street to the clinic.

Whitney got wobbly about halfway down the block. He scooped her up in his arms and hurried to the clinic. To see Ashley. Again.

* * * * *

Ashley looked up at the sound of the clinic's door opening at the end of a long afternoon. A bare-chested Will came rushing through with Whitney in his arms. "Whit needs help." Will's voice was laced with urgency and a touch of fear.

Ashley hurried forward. "What happened?"

"She cut her hand on some glass. It's bleeding pretty badly."

"Come this way and let me look at it." Ashley led the way to a room and Will quickly settled Whitney on the exam table.

"You doing okay, Whitney?" Ashley crossed the room and carefully unwrapped the blood soaked t-shirt from around Whitney's hand.

That explained the bare-chested Will.

"Just got a bit woozy. I'm not great with the sight of

blood."

"Okay, just lie back and let me look at this." Ashley cleaned the wound and applied pressure again, always cognizant of Will hovering right behind her. She stepped back and bumped into him.

"Oh, sorry." She motioned to the gauze she'd applied to Whitney's wound. "Here, you hold this and I'll get the suture kit."

He brushed past her without a word and did as she asked, holding a layer of gauze against the wound. She left the room to get the supplies and returned to find Will leaning over Whitney, talking softly to her.

"Gonna be okay, sis. You'll see. It will be over before you know it."

"I'm fine." Whitney tried to convince her brother, her words filled with false bravado.

"I can see by the gray look on your face that you're doing fantastic," Will countered wryly.

Ashley rolled a tray beside the exam table and angled the light down on Whitney's hand. "You could sit up, but if you're feeling faint, I think it might be better if you stay where you are."

"She's not getting up." Will answered for her.

"I've got her now, if you want to go sit down in the waiting room." *And take that bare skin of yours with you.*

"I'm not leaving." He grabbed a chair and rolled it over by the table. "I'll stay out of your way."

Ashley stitched the wound while Will talked to his

sister constantly, keeping her occupied and her mind off the procedure. "You're okay. Look at me, not Ashley. She knows what she's doing. You just look at me. Hey, no more fainting."

"I'm fine, Willie."

"I know you are. You're doing great." Will pushed a lock of hair away from his sister's face with a gentle sweep of his strong hand. Ashely had always admired the way he was so protective of his sister, always taking care of her. It was obvious that hadn't changed over the years.

She finished up and dressed the wound. "All finished. You feel like sitting up now?"

"I think so."

Will carefully helped his sister sit on the exam table.

"Just sit there for a few minutes and let's see how you do. The numbing agent is going to wear off in about an hour or so. I'm going to send you home with some pain pills. You won't be able to use that hand for a while either. You need to give those stitches time to heal."

Whitney let out a long sigh, but Ashely was glad to see a bit of color coming back to her face.

"I have Dad to take care of. I can't do that one-handed."

"I'm sure your brother will help you with Warren."

Whitney looked at Will questioningly. "Willie?"

Ashley could feel the tension radiating from Will's rigid frame. He looked at his sister for a long moment, then did a slow nod. "I'll help. You just take it easy and don't use that hand."

Will turned to Ashley, and she couldn't avoid the electricity that flashed between them. "Can you watch Whitney while I go get her car? There's no way she's going to walk back to the cottage."

"Yes, she can stay here with me. I think getting the car is a good idea." Ashley took a step back, away from him, away from his bare chest. "If you want, I'll get you a scrub top to wear."

Will looked down and seemed to suddenly realize he was standing there bare to the waist. "Thanks. I'll take you up on that."

She hurried away to get the scrubs to cover the tanned muscles on Will's very fit torso, not that she noticed it. Much.

* * * * *

Will slipped on the scrub top Ashley handed him and escaped the clinic. The fresh air wrapped around him and helped soothe his jangled nerves. His adrenaline had been on overdrive from the moment he saw Whitney on the floor among all the broken glass, and it hadn't helped he had to sit beside Ashley while she worked on Whit. How much was one man supposed to handle in a day?

Oh, and let's add in he'd promised his sister he'd help take care of Warren.

Great.

He had to admit he'd been impressed with Ashley. So efficient and professional. Gentle with Whitney, explaining what she was doing, giving the numbing agent time to work before starting into the procedure. Ashley had been born to be a doctor. She was a natural healer, always wanting to fix people or help them. He'd had no doubt she'd find a way to pay for medical school. It's not like either of them had any money when they were growing up. They'd lived in that run-down apartment complex, and both of them had held jobs as soon as possible. Ashley had studied hard and been an honor student. Will had barely gotten by in high school except for math. He'd shone in math class. Well, until he had to drop out of high school his senior year so he could make enough to support Whitney when their dad had barely brought in any money, and what he did, he spent on booze.

He paused in front of Whitney's cottage, ordering himself to go inside and get her car keys. But in order to do that, he'd probably run into Warren. He sucked in a deep breath and tugged open the door.

"Hello, son." His father sat in a chair by the window with sunshine streaming in all around him. He didn't look like a man who needed help.

Will ignored the way Warren called him son. "I just came to get Whit's keys. She's had an accident."

His father's eyes filled with alarm. "Is she okay?"

"Got some stitches. She needs to take it easy for a few days and not use her hand."

"Where is she now?"

"She's at the clinic. I'm going to go pick her up. She's in no condition to walk back here."

"She always has a hard time at the sight of blood." His father nodded his head.

Will was surprised his father knew that little detail about Whitney. Will had been the one to bandage up her skinned knees and elbows.

He fished the car keys from the bowl on the counter. "We'll be back soon." He turned and fled the cottage.

He was always escaping from somewhere on this ill-fated return to Indigo Bay.

* * * * *

"You doing okay?" Ashley looked over at Whitney after she finished making some notes in the chart.

"Yes, I'm fine. Will is overreacting as usual."

"You were pale as a ghost when he brought you in here." Ashley cocked her head to one side. "Thought I might lose you to a faint when I started stitching you up, too."

"Well, I feel fine now. I really should go to the shop and clean up all the glass."

"That's not going to happen. You need to go home and put your hand up and take it easy. It's going to hurt a bit this evening."

"So, when a doc admits it's going to hurt a bit, it means it's going to really ache, doesn't it?

"It might smart some." Ashley closed the chart and leaned back in the chair, stretching her legs out in front of her.

"So... I guess I should have told you Willie was coming into town." Whitney drummed her fingers of her good hand on the exam table.

"That would have been nice."

"I didn't really think he'd come when I called, then he was here like the next day."

"When has Will ever refused anything you asked of him?"

"Point taken." Whitney started to get down from the exam table.

Ashley sprang to her feet. "If you want down, let me steady you at least." She helped Whitney to a more comfortable chair.

"I'm sorry it caught you by surprise, Ashley. I am. I should have made a point to call and tell you. I've just been so overwhelmed with this tax problem at the shop and Dad's accident. Not to mention I decided Dad should move in while he recovers."

"It's okay. I understand. I was just... surprised to see him here."

"About as surprised as he was to see you, I imagine." Whitney settled more comfortably in the chair. "I never could figure out why you two broke up. You always seemed to enjoy each other's company. It was like you were best friends."

"We were. Then it turned into the whole boyfriend, girlfriend thing. But we wanted different things. I was set on medical school and had things planned out. Will just seems to drift through life. He even dropped out of high school—"

"Whit, you ready to go?" Will stood in the doorway.

His eyes flashed with anger and maybe a little hurt? How could that be? After all these years? Was he still hurt and mad at her?

"I'm ready." Whitney started to stand and Will rushed over to help her.

"We should take Ashley home, too. She can ride with us." Whit leaned against her brother.

"No."

"No."

Will and Ashley said the word at the same time.

"I have some things to finish up here at the clinic. I'll walk back when I'm finished."

"And I need to get you home and settled in." Will took his sister's arm and started to lead her out of the exam room.

"We could wait for her."

"No, you go on." The last thing Ashley needed was to spend more time with Will. Even if he did have a shirt on now.

Chapter Five

Ashley headed out to walk to work early the next day. She'd risen with a bundle of nervous energy and figured she'd put that to good use by cleaning out the storage room at the clinic before the day got too busy. As she walked past Coastal Creations, she saw the door was wide open, and she peeked inside.

Will knelt on the floor, his head bent, sorting through the mess, carefully picking up pieces of jewelry and placing them on a tray. Before she could stop herself— *like any rational person would do*—she entered the shop. "Let me help you."

Will looked up, startled. "Ah… no, I'm okay. I've got this."

"I'll help, I have time." Ashley knelt beside him. "If we don't get this picked up, you know Whitney will be here doing it herself."

"That's the truth. I had to make her promise to stay

home this morning. I told her I'd get everything picked up, and if she feels up to it, she can come in this afternoon and order me around and tell me where to put all the jewelry items for display."

Will gently placed a broken necklace in the tray. "I don't know when she'll have enough use of her hand to fix these or create more. She's going to be even more stressed."

"You were always good with your hands. Maybe she can show you or tell you how to fix them."

She stared at his hands for a moment with his long fingers on the strong, calloused hand. She tore her glance away from her scrutiny and her speculation about whether his hands would still be unbelievably gentle when he touched her.

Not that he'd touch her now.

"Maybe." He looked doubtful.

Maybe, what? What had she asked him?

"But, she's the creative one." He continued to talk to her like she was actually paying attention and could figure out what he was saying to her.

Right, she'd said he could help Whitney with the jewelry repairs.

With his hands.

She tore her look away yet again.

"It looks like you have the jewelry pieces picked up. I'll go grab a broom and we'll sweep up the rest of the glass." She stood, carefully picking her way through the broken shards, and headed to the back office. She knew her way around Coastal Creations because she'd often meet Whitney after work and they'd sit and talk before they walked home, or they'd go out for a quick bite to eat or an occasional girls' night on the town.

Those nights would be over until Will left town. How many more days did he say he was staying?

* * * * *

Will watched as Ashley gracefully rose to her feet and headed to the back office. He sank back on his heels, trying to catch his breath. Ashley showed up every time he turned around in this town and he didn't like to admit it shook him at each encounter.

She returned with the broom and started to sweep up the glass while he sorted the jewelry onto two trays, broken pieces on one and intact pieces on the other. The sunlight streamed through the front window and set Ashley's auburn hair on fire. It drifted down around her shoulders now, but yesterday at the clinic she'd had it pulled back in a fancy braid. He liked it better down like this.

Not that it really mattered to him one way or the other, of course.

She worked efficiently and swept up the last of the glass. She stood and let the light shine on the floor, looking carefully, searching for stray pieces of glass. She leaned down and reached out with her slender fingers, gathering a few pieces she'd missed. "I think I've got it all now."

"Thanks for the help."

"You're welcome."

"Here, I'll take those." He reached for the broom and dustpan.

"Oh. Here." She handed them to him and looked questioningly into his eyes.

He stepped back a pace or two, giving some much needed distance between them.

She dropped her hands to her side. "I was planning on stopping by tonight to check on Warren and Whitney, if that's okay."

He bobbed his head in agreement. How could he say no to that?

She nodded in reply, then turned and left without another word. He saw her pass by the front window, leaving him alone in the shop.

How was it that he always was feeling so alone in Indigo Bay?

A shadow filled the doorway again a few moments later, and for a brief second he thought Ashley had returned.

"Willie Layton, is that you?" Lucille Sanderson stood in the doorway in her precisely ironed dress, looking exactly like she had ten years ago, or twenty years ago for that matter.

Lucille entered the shop. "I heard you were back in town."

"I am." He glanced each direction to see if he could escape. The last thing he needed was an inquisition from Lucille.

"And your sister got hurt, poor thing."

That was quick. But then Lucille always knew everything about everyone and was always willing to spread whatever news she uncovered.

"She'll be fine."

"And here she is taking care of poor Warren, too. How will she manage?"

"Whitney will figure it out." No way he was going to say he was here helping or even imply his sister needed help. No telling what that would turn into by the time Lucille had twisted it around to spread her gossip.

"Well, you be sure to have her just ask for any little thing if she needs it. I know her business has really grown, well just look how she was able to afford a decent place on Seaside Boulevard and move out of that tacky apartment she'd been living in. That's not a nice part of town for a woman to live in, you know. We're so glad she moved."

He wondered who *we* were.

"Anyway, I just wanted to check when I saw the front door was open to Coastal Creations, knowing she was injured and all."

"Thanks for checking." He said with hardly a hint of sincerity in his voice, not that he figured Lucille would notice.

"Well, of course. I wouldn't want anything to happen to poor Whitney's shop."

Poor Whitney, poor Warren. How about poor Will dealing with all of this?

"Well, I need to run along. Have a meeting with the Ashland Belle Society for the festival this weekend. You're coming, right? Everyone in town will be there."

"We'll see." Not a snowball's chance in Hades he'd be there.

"Good, we'll see you then." There was that *we* thing again.

* * * * *

Willie stood in Whitney's small kitchen working on the one dinner he knew how to make, spaghetti. Whitney had gone to rest for a bit after a brief foray to her shop this afternoon.

That hadn't turned out like he planned. She tried to fix some pieces of jewelry and he kept yelling at her to stop using her hand. They'd both ended up frustrated, and he'd brought her home. He wasn't getting any brother of the year awards this week.

He stood at the stove and stirred the spaghetti sauce, looking out the window at the view of the beach, lost in thought. If he'd walk down the beach just a bit, he'd get to the place where he used to meet Ashley. They called it their place, but it was actually a grove of palm trees on the property of some snowbird owners who only came to Indigo Bay for six weeks or so in the wintertime. The

46

home had a gazebo, partially hidden from the house and the beach by overgrown bushes. That was where they'd sneak off to meet all those years ago. They'd pretend they weren't two of the poorest kids at school, living in a horrible apartment complex. Ashley's father had been a custodian at the high school. Ashley had gotten teased about that, but she always acknowledged him when she saw him and would often walk to school with him. He wondered if her father was still working the same job.

He turned at the sound of Warren rolling into the kitchen.

"Can I help with anything, son?"

"I'm not sure why every time you speak to me, you need to add the word son." Okay, so he wasn't going to get son of the year either, though he hardly considered Warren a father.

"I'm sorry." Warren looked at him, and Will turned to stare at the sauce again.

"I know you're angry with me, and you have every right to be. I was a terrible father to both of you."

Will didn't even dignify that with an answer.

"I was just so lost when Maria died. I loved her so much. She was my whole world." His father rolled further into the kitchen.

Will spun towards him. "That much was obvious. That *she* was your whole world. Because you conveniently forgot you had two children who needed you. You know we lost our *mother*, you didn't just lose your wife."

47

"I know that. I'm so sorry for how I reacted. How long it took me to... well, to change. I know it's too late to get back all that time. I know the burden of so much fell on your shoulders, and you were way too young to take on that responsibility."

"There was no one else to take it on." Will's words were edged in ice and resentment.

"I admire all you did to hold things together for Whitney. I can't ever thank you enough for that. I can't repay you for all you did."

"I don't want *anything* from you." Will turned his attention to stirring the sauce that didn't need stirring.

"I don't expect you to ever forgive me, son." Warren paused, looked at Will, and continued. "But I hope we can somehow come to a truce of some kind where we can just move on from this point onward. For Whitney's sake if for no other reason."

"So, I'm just supposed to forget the past? Forget all I gave up because you couldn't be bothered to be a dad and support us? Forget how you weren't there for me, for us, when we needed you most?"

"I don't think you'll ever forget that, and I'm not asking you to." His father's words were spoken in a low voice. "I would just like to... get along civilly, if possible. For Whitney's sake. Can you do that, s—? Ah, can you do that?"

"I honestly don't know, Warren."

A knock at the door saved him from having to

continue the conversation. He brushed past Warren and went to answer the door.

"Ashley."

"Hi, I just wanted to pop in and check on my patients. It's your lucky day to have a doctor who makes house calls."

His lucky day. Right.

Whitney came walking out of her bedroom. "Thought I heard your voice. Come in. Sit down for a bit."

"I won't stay long, I just wanted to check on you and Warren."

"I'm fit as a fiddle." Warren rolled into the family room. "Getting better every day."

"Well, don't overdo it. You'll start physical therapy next week."

"Looking forward to it. I want to get my strength back and some stability."

"You'll get there." Ashley smiled at Warren and turned to Whitney. "Any pain today?"

"Not too bad. Aches a bit."

"Because she tried to overdo it at the shop this afternoon." Will rolled his eyes.

"There's so much to do. I can't be out of commission for very long."

"You should take it easy for a few more days and try not to use that hand much. Give it time to heal up a bit." Ashley gave Whitney a listen-to-your-doctor look.

Will was pretty certain Whitney would still do as she

pleased.

"Hey, Ash, why don't you stay for dinner? Willie made his famous spaghetti." Whitney grinned at Will, and he shot her an are-you-crazy? glare.

"Oh, I don't want to intrude."

"Not at all. We'd love to have you." Warren joined in on the invitation as if he had any right to be asking people to dinner here in Whitney's cottage.

Ashley looked directly at Will, and he drew in a deep breath of oxygen-less air. "Okay. Sure, stay if you want. I made plenty."

The night couldn't get much better than this. Not only was he going to be forced to sit down to his first family dinner in he didn't know how many years, but Ashley was going to join them.

Great. Just great.

* * * * *

Ashley helped Will with the place settings. The table was in a small alcove with a bench along one side and a view of the ocean. The table was small, barely enough room for the four of them.

Warren rolled his chair up to the table and Whitney sat beside him. That left the bench seat for Ashley and Will. He walked in carrying a big pot with the spaghetti sauce, and she watched him pause when he saw the seating arrangements. He set the container on a hot pad and disappeared back into the kitchen.

He came out with the bowl of spaghetti noodles in one

hand and a tray of toasty bread in the other. She slipped onto the bench seat and made room for Will.

"Oh, forgot the salad. It's just salad in a bag. Even I can make that." He disappeared yet again.

Ashley wondered how many trips he could make back into the kitchen to avoid sitting next to her, which was just fine by her.

He came back with a bowl of caesar salad and set it on the table. He stood at the end of the bench.

"Sit down, Willie. Dinner will get cold." Whitney motioned to the bench with her fork.

He slipped onto the bench beside Ashley, bumping gently against her arm. He quickly slid away from her, putting inches of space between them, but it did little to stop the thumping of her heart.

Whitney carried the majority of the conversation, seemingly oblivious to Will's one-word answers to any questions she asked.

Will reached for the butter at the exact same moment Ashley did, and their fingers brushed. He jerked his hand back as if he'd been burned in a fire. She took the butter and placed a pat on her plate and handed it to him. He took it from her, careful to make sure their hands didn't touch.

"So, Ashley, you going to the festival this weekend?"

"I'm planning to." She hoped if she joined in with some of the town's activities, that maybe the town would begin to accept her a little more.

"You should go with us. I'm going to have a booth with my jewelry."

"I… ah…"

"Dad's going, aren't you, Dad?"

"I don't want to be a burden."

"Nonsense. There's a wooden walkway out to the gazebo. We can push you out there, can't we, Willie?"

"I wasn't planning on going." Will folded his arms across his chest.

"Sure you are. The whole town will be there."

Ashley saw the deer-in-the-headlights look in Will's eyes.

"Willie will help me get you to the gazebo, Dad. It will do you good to get out of the house."

"I don't want to be any trouble."

"You're no trouble, Dad, really. It will be fun."

"I'm sure Willie wants to be there to yell at me if he think I'm overdoing it, anyway." Whitney grinned at her brother.

"Okay, I'll go. But only to keep you in line. And I'm going to be dragging you home if you start overdoing it. I mean it."

"Sure, whatever you say. I always listen to my big brother." Whitney laughed.

"As if," Will muttered under his breath.

"Well, I'll meet you there, Whitney. How about that?" Ashley wasn't going to commit to any more time with Will than absolutely necessary.

"Sounds great." Whitney returned to eating her spaghetti with gusto, pleased she'd gotten everyone to do as she wished. As usual.

*   *   *   *   *

Ashley had insisted on helping Will clean up from dinner. Whitney's tiny kitchen seemed to grow smaller by the minute as Ashley worked beside him. She'd wash a dish and hand it to him to dry.

How the heck had they'd gotten so many dishes dirty? He was sure the dishwashing torture was never going to end.

He finally placed the last dish back into the cabinet. "All finished."

Whitney popped her head into the kitchen. "Great, you're done. Willie, why don't you walk Ashely home?"

"There's no need. I'm just right next door." Ashley quickly jumped in.

"Of course he'll see you to your door. It's how he was raised."

Will rolled his eyes. Who could refuse Whitney anything? "Come on, Ashley, I'll walk the twenty steps it takes to get you over to your cottage."

They slipped outside into the cool night air. The tangy scent of the sea surrounded them. Moonlight spilled down on the waves as they rolled to shore.

"It's a beautiful night." Ashley paused and looked up at the stars.

"It is." He'd give her that. Whitney was lucky to live on

the beach now, with the vast vista of stars, instead of the tiny slivers of sky they had been able to see out of the tiny windows in their childhood apartments. Of course, he'd tried to stay out of the apartment as much as possible when he was young. He'd escape to the beach whenever he got the chance.

"So do you like living back in Indigo Bay?" He was surprised the question just slipped out. What difference did it make to him what Ashley liked or disliked these days?

"I do. I enjoy working at the clinic, though I'm having a tough time winning the townspeople over. They miss Doc Browning. I'm not sure I'll ever live up to his reputation. I'm trying to keep things running smoothly until he returns."

"You were good with Whitney."

"Thanks. She was easy. We'd already become friends. The rest of the town? Well, that's a harder sell. I'm not sure they'll ever think of me as someone other than that poor girl from the wrong side of town."

"You'll win them over, Ash." He was certain she would, it just might take some time.

Ashley stopped at the base of the steps to her cottage. "Well, here I am. Home all safe and sound."

Will grinned. "Yep, all the way from that deck right there to this one."

She smiled back at him. "Thanks for escorting me to my door. Very gallant of you."

"I'm a very gallant kind of guy." *Where was this easy banter coming from?*

"Well, I better go in. I have an early day tomorrow."

"Goodnight, Ash."

"Night, Will."

He watched while she unlocked the door and slipped inside. The cottage was quickly flooded with light, and she turned and gave him a little wave through the window.

He stared at his hand, raised in an answering wave to hers. She closed the blinds and just like that, she was gone from his sight.

Chapter Six

The next morning Will stood in front of the coffeemaker as it gurgled and hissed its way through brewing a pot. He wished he could silence the noise before it woke up Warren and Whitney.

When the machine finally finished its slow torture, he poured himself a steaming mug of coffee and slipped outside to the deck. He wrapped his palms around the mug and leaned against the railing, watching the sky lighten and waiting for the sun to break through the early-morning clouds. This he'd missed. Sunrise over the ocean. Belle Island sits on the west coast of Florida, so it provides sunsets over the ocean, not sunrises. Sunsets were great and all that, but he was drawn to sunrises, maybe because not many people were stirring yet. The new day stretched out before him, a new beginning, a new slate to draw on, each and every day.

He glanced over at Ashley's cottage and saw her

nestled on a chair, wrapped in a blanket, staring at the ocean. Without thinking, he stepped off of Whitney's deck and crossed the distance to Ashley, another sunrise lover.

"Morning." He spoke softly as he climbed the stairs to her deck.

She looked up and smiled at him, as if all those years had just slipped away and they were back in time, when things were easy between them, back when... she loved him. "Morning, Will. I see you still like to get up and watch the sunrise."

"I do." He rested a hip against her deck railing. "There's nothing like a sunrise over the ocean."

"You'll get no argument from me there."

They watched in silence as the sky turned pink and rays of sunlight broke through splits in the clouds. Suddenly the sun burst above the horizon and spilled its golden light across the waves.

"Ah..." Ashley's voice was a whisper.

He turned to see the golden light bathing her features. She seemed so relaxed, in sharp contrast to the usual determined and intense look that usually adorned her face. She looked up and caught him staring at her.

She smiled a tentative smile. "I've missed these sunrises with you. I don't think anyone else ever appreciated them like we do."

"Maybe not." He shrugged.

"Are you happy now, Will?"

Her question caught him off guard. Happy? He guessed so. "Sure."

"I'm glad. I know we ended... badly. It was messy and hard and just... well, it was hard to finish senior year of high school without you. I was so disappointed when you dropped out."

And she'd made that point abundantly clear. She'd yelled at him when he told her he was dropping out. She hadn't wanted to hear his excuses, as far as she was concerned there was no excuse. She had plans for her life, and he didn't. She boiled their whole relationship down to that. He'd been so hurt and angry that he'd just walked away in stony silence. Besides, he'd promised Whitney that he'd never tell anyone that Warren went missing so often, and he'd kept that promise.

So, he'd just done what he had to do, left school to pick up a second job. Whit was six years younger, and he'd been determined to give her the most normal life he could. He also was determined to never let anyone have that kind of power over him. The power that when they left him, it crushed him.

He should remember that and quit staring at Ashley in the sunlight. She looked beautiful, and the sight of her took his breath away.

Ashley stood and turned to him, oblivious to the turmoil racing through him. "I'm glad you came over to share the sunrise with me today."

"I am, too." And he realized with a start he *was* glad

Kay Correll

he'd come over. He felt connected to her again in some way. Sunrise had always been their special time when they'd slip out to meet before the complications of their lives drifted down around them.

But he wasn't sure he wanted to feel connected to Ashley again.

She smiled at him and held out her empty coffee mug. "All gone. I better finish getting ready for work."

He nodded and watched while she slipped back into her cottage. He jogged the steps back to Whitney's and took one last look at the sunrise. He went inside to start breakfast for Warren and Whitney before his sister had a chance to even think about making it herself. And by making breakfast he meant pouring some cereal and making some toast.

* * * * *

Will spent the next few days arguing with Whitney, imploring her to take it easy and quit using her hand, as if Whitney was going to listen to anyone when she had her mind set.

"Willie, do you think you should head back to Belle Island?" Whitney finally blurted out in frustration as they sat in the office of her shop and he'd told her yet one more time to put down the jewelry piece she was clumsily trying to put together.

"Nice try. Who would nag you to slow down and rest your hand? Besides, I haven't finished sorting out your books yet. They're a mess." He set down another stack of invoices.

"I know." His sister finally put down the shell and wire she was working with. "And I know you mean well with the ever constant, overboard, annoying nagging."

"Tell me how you really feel." Will grinned at his sister.

"I'm not used to asking for help or feeling so... dependent."

"You're getting better. Ashley said you'd be able to use your hand sparingly this weekend at the festival." The festival he'd agreed to go to and take his father. A long sigh escaped him.

"Will, can we talk?"

"Isn't that what we're doing?"

"No, I mean seriously talk."

Will looked at his sister and recognized the expression. She had that I'm-going-to-get-my-way look on her face. "We can talk, but that doesn't mean I have to agree with whatever it is you're going to say."

Whitney pushed back her hair—with her good hand—and nodded. "I don't think I've ever thanked you enough for all you did for me when we were growing up. You gave up so much so that I could have a normal life. I lived in fear that some scary social-services lady was going to swoop down and take me away from you. But you always made sure things ran smoothly and no one knew how bad Dad really was."

"I'd do the same thing again for you, Whit. You know

that."

"Well, I want to do something for you now, to pay you back."

"You don't owe me anything. It was just the life we were handed."

"No, listen to me, Willie. Really listen." The intent look on her face made him sit quietly and let her have her say.

"I made a lot of money off Coastal Creations."

"I know, and I'm proud of you."

Whitney sent him a let-me-finish glare. "I want you to take some of the money. It's the least I can do. I wouldn't be where I am now if you hadn't given up so much for me."

"Whit, I don't need your money."

"But I want to make your life easier. I have my shop, my beach house, I have everything I need."

"I have everything I need, too."

"But I know you work long hours bartending at the Lucky Duck."

"I love bartending there, or I wouldn't do it."

"But it would make me feel better if I could finally do something for you. Look at you. You've taken two weeks off work, so you're not earning a thing, and you've come here to help me out."

Will got up and walked over to his sister. "Whit, seriously, I don't need your money. I'm doing fine." He paused and looked at his sister for a long moment. "I... I actually bought The Lucky Duck last year."

"You what?" Whitney's eyes widen. "You didn't tell me that."

"I'm telling you now." Will hadn't told anyone he'd bought the tavern. He wasn't sure many people on Belle Island even knew he owned it. He was just their trusty bartender, and he liked it that way. Maybe it was because it surprised him that he could afford to buy the place and was afraid it would be taken away from him.

"How did you do that? I mean, save up enough to do that?"

"Well, you know how I've always been good with numbers?"

"Yes, that's why I asked you to help me with the books." Whitney stared at him intently.

"Well, it turns out I'm also pretty good with investments."

"How good?"

"Really good."

Whitney tossed him a wide grin. "Well, that's great news."

"I was just getting ready to offer to help you out with starting up your jewelry business when that whole social media thing went viral and your business took off. So I took the money I'd set aside to help you and invested in part ownership of the Lucky Duck. Then last year I bought out the other owner, and it's all mine."

"You never cease to surprise me." Whitney set down a

shell she'd been fiddling with. "I'm really proud of you."

"I'm proud of you, too."

"We've really come a long way from the dingy old apartment and our old lives, haven't we?"

"With no help from Dad." Will was sorry the minute the words slipped out of his mouth.

"Don't be like that. He did the best he could. He's changed now."

"So you say."

"Are you ever going to forgive him?"

"I honestly don't know, Whit."

"I know you gave up more than I had to. I know you resent that, and I don't blame you. You had to be an adult at age fifteen, and you were basically supporting us by the time you were eighteen. Well, even before that when Mom was so sick." Whitney looked at him with a sad expression clouding her face. "I miss Mom. Even after all this time. I still want her here. Talking to me. Letting me help her in the kitchen. Do you still miss her?"

"Every single day, Whit. Every single day."

His sister sat in silence for a moment then looked directly into his eyes. "But I still hope you can work something out with Dad. Find a way to... Well, I miss having a family."

That comment stung. He'd always considered him and Whit a family, just the two of them.

Will looked at his sister suspiciously. "So, did you decide you needed this help with your books *right now*, because you knew Warren would be at your cottage and you wanted us to spend time together?"

Whitney blushed. "Well, I *do* need help getting all the accounting mess sorted out. I have that audit coming up."

Will let out a long whoosh of air. "Whitney Layton, you are the most frustrating sister I've ever had."

"And your favorite." Whitney grinned.

"That, too."

Chapter Seven

The day of the festival graced the town with perfect weather, sunny and warm, but not too hot. Early that morning Willie helped Whitney set up a booth. The table was covered in a crisp white linen cloth, and Whitney carefully arranged a display of her jewelry. She stood back and admired her handiwork.

"I think that's it." She set a box under the table then turned to Will. "Can you go back and get Dad now?"

Will couldn't think of any other way to stall. He might as well go get Warren and bring him to the festival. *Why had he agreed to do that?*

"You could poke your head in at Ashley's and see if she wants a ride, too."

"She said she'd meet you here."

"It would be the neighborly thing to do."

"Whitney, how about you concentrate on selling your jewelry—the display looks really nice by the way—and

I'll worry about what I'm going to do or not do." He turned and stalked away, threading his way through the gathering crowds of people. He wasn't really angry with Whitney, even though she did have a way of bossing him around, and he usually did as she wished. She had a big heart and always thought the best of everyone, unlike the cynical person he'd become.

He slowed and strolled through the park situated at the far end of Indigo Bay. The air was filled with the tantalizing hints of fried food and a lingering aroma of baked goods. A large tent had been set up with a sign proclaiming the biggest baking contest in all of South Carolina.

Booths were filled with craft items, antiques, every kind of food imaginable, from jams and jellies to pies to cookies. He considered stopping and buying a sweet roll and a cup of coffee. He deserved a break before heading back to get Warren. But guilt overcame him, and he headed to Whitney's car to go back to the cottage.

Warren was waiting on the front deck. "I guess I'm a bit more excited to get out and about than I thought. I appreciate you hauling me over to the festival."

"It's not a problem." It *was* a problem, but he was doing it anyway.

Will turned the wheelchair around and slowly lowered Warren down the two steps of the deck. He pushed the chair up to the car and looked at Warren. His father started to push off the arms of the chair and stand,

and the wheelchair began to roll backward.

Will instinctively reached out to steady Warren. The man's hands grasped at Will's forearms and Will held him securely. The shock of the actual touch of his father… after so many, many years brought Will to a standstill. He couldn't remember the last physical contact he'd had with his father, a hug, a handshake, or even a pat on the shoulder for a job well done? Nothing came to mind. Nothing at all.

His father looked him right in the eyes. "Thanks, s—Will."

Will nodded, because there was no way he could form any semblance of coherent speech at the moment. He leveraged his father into the front passenger seat and slowly walked around to the back of the vehicle. He collapsed the wheelchair and wrestled it into the trunk. He slammed the trunk a little too forcefully and jerked open the driver's door. He slid into the seat and started the car, still not saying a word.

When they got to the festival, Will helped Warren out of the car and settled him back in the wheelchair. Once again Warren's hands grasped at him as he clumsily transferred the man from the car to the wheelchair. Will let out a grunt when Warren was settled. He'd had no idea transferring someone to and from a wheelchair took so much work.

He pushed the chair over to the wooden walkway and crossed over to the gazebo. "You going to be okay here?"

Warren nodded.

"You want to stay in the wheelchair? Or I could help you into one of those Adirondack chairs."

"If you don't mind helping me, I'd love to get out of this thing and sit in one of those chairs. They look comfortable, and I'm getting sick and tired of being tied to this contraption."

Will locked the wheels on the wheelchair—he was at least learning a bit about the mechanics of transferring Warren from place to place—and helped his father stand. Warren leaned heavily on Will as he led him to his seat. "You all good?"

"I'm good."

"Hi." Will turned at the sound of Ashley's voice. A voice that he thought he'd forgotten, but these last few days brought back the knowledge of every little timbre and lilt of each word she spoke.

She wore a simple print sundress and sandals. Her auburn hair drifted around her shoulders. She looked just... beautiful.

Not that he noticed.

She smiled at Warren. "Glad to see you made it. It will do you good to get out."

"It is nice. I feel like I've been stuck inside for weeks."

"You have been. It's been a long recovery." Ashley rested her hand on Warren's shoulder. "Are you comfortable here?"

"Yes, I'm good." Warren smiled at Ashley. "I don't

need fussing over. Why don't you two go walk around the festival, get something to eat, have fun?"

"I... Will, do you want to wander around a bit?" Ashley looked at him with a you-don't-have-to-say-yes expression.

"Ashley, there you are." A woman who looked familiar to him, but he couldn't quite place, walked up with a young girl in tow.

Who was she? Someone from their school days. Her name was on the tip of his tongue.

"Hello, Vicki." Ashley gave him the hint he needed.

Vicki Holloway. How could he have forgotten her? She'd been a constant source of friction when they were in school.

"I told you no one calls me Vicki anymore. It's Victoria." The woman tossed her blonde hair behind her shoulder.

"You remember Will, don't you? He went to school with us." Ashley tilted her head towards him.

Vicki stared at him, with narrowed eyes and pursed lips. "I... yes. I think so." Then she promptly turned away from him and squared off with Ashley. There just wasn't another term he could think of to describe how the woman faced Ashley.

"Mia here isn't feeling very well. Are you sure you didn't miss something when I brought her in to see you?"

"I think she had the virus that was going around, but we could go to the clinic again now if you want me to check her out again. Is she running a fever?"

"No, she's just not her usual self. And I don't have time to go to the clinic. I'm in charge of the baking contest and I need to get over to the tent."

Ashley turned to Mia. "Are you feeling okay?"

"I'm just tired." The girl looked down at her feet as she answered.

"I bet you are. It takes a while to get over being sick."

Warren smiled at the girl. "You know what? I have to just sit here. I'm not up to walking around. You want to stay with me while your mother goes and works at the baking contest? I bet Will and Ashley could bring you back a snow cone."

Ashley knelt down at Mia's level. "How about that? You want to stay here in the shade where it's cooler? You want to stay with us?"

The girl nodded then looked down again.

Vicki looked at them all skeptically. "I suppose that would be okay." She nodded towards Warren. "I know Mr. Layton here from church."

Will felt his mouth gape open. She knew Warren from church? Since when?

Vicki ignored Will's astonishment. "They really need me at the baking contest." Her look of skepticism quickly changed to one of relief. "Yes, that would be fine."

Vicki hadn't changed much. Still thinking of herself. Will was surprised she'd just leave her daughter with them, though Ashley was a doctor, so who better to leave a sick kid with? Oh, and with a man she knew from her *church*. Will shook his head.

"I'll be back after the contest is over. It may be a while."

"That's fine. We'll keep an eye on Mia." Ashley put her hand on the girl's shoulder.

Vicki spun on her heels—who wore heels to a festival like this?—and left without so much as a kiss or hug for her daughter.

* * * * *

"So, would you like a snow cone?" Ashley knelt in front of Mia.

"Yes, please." Mia nodded.

"How about we play some cards? You want to play Go Fish while Ashely and Will find you a snow cone?" Warren looked at Mia.

"You want to play with me?" The little girl's eyes widen.

"Yep. Sure do. I love playing Go Fish. It's my favorite card game." Warren winked at the girl and she grinned.

Mia sat in the chair next to Warren and Will pulled a low table over between them.

"Can you reach into the pocket on the back of my wheelchair? I always keep a book and a deck of cards in there."

Will walked over to the wheelchair, retrieved the deck of cards, and handed them to Warren. "Here you go."

Warren slipped off the rubber band encircling the

deck and held out the cards to Mia. "You want to deal them?"

"Me?"

"Yep. Seven cards to each of us."

Mia reached eagerly for the cards. She concentrated while she dealt. "One for you. One for me. One for you. One for me."

Ashley smiled as she watched Mia deal the cards.

Warren looked up and grinned. "I think we're all set here. Why don't you two walk around a bit, then bring a snow cone back for my card partner?"

"Okay, we won't be long." Ashley watched Mia carefully try to sort her cards into some kind of order in her small hands. "You all good, Mia?"

Mia nodded then bent back to concentrate on her cards.

Ashley and Will crossed the gazebo and out onto the sandy beach. She raised her face to the warm sunshine and let it bathe over her. She loved this time of year before the summer crowds, though the festival certainly had attracted its share of tourists today.

"You were really good with Mia." Will turned to face her.

"She seems like a sweet kid."

"She seems like a kid whose mother doesn't have much time for her."

"You're probably right. But then, Vicki's always been like that, hasn't she? It's always all about Vicki. Mia sure perked up when your father asked if she wanted to play cards."

"That kind of surprised me." Will's face scrunched into a scowl.

"That Mia wanted to play cards?"

"No, that Warren had the cards and offered to play with her. I just… well, it's not like he ever played cards with me that I can remember."

"He was gone a lot on business, wasn't he?" Ashley didn't know why Will was so angry with Warren. His father had travelled frequently and didn't seem to be around much when they were growing up, but he'd probably done the best he could as a single father. Will hadn't talked about him much when they were younger.

"He was gone quite a bit." Will's voice was flat.

Ashley decided to change the subject. "So, which way do you want to go?" Ashley looked at the rows of art, crafts, food, and a big area that was like a flea market filled with who knew what.

"You choose."

"This way, then." Ashley headed down a row of arts and crafts stopping at a few booths here and there. Will trailed along with her, fairly uninterested until they reached a booth filled with every tool imaginable. She laughed as she followed him along the narrow pathways of the large tent. "I don't even know what some of these tools are."

"You don't have a multi-use knife? Look, it even has a

corkscrew." Will held up what looked like a massive pocket knife. "Or, here, a solar-powered charger for your phone, complete with a suction cup so you can put it on your window when you fly in a plane. You probably need this. Great for long trips." Will grinned.

"No doubt it is." She laughed.

They walked on and an easiness fell between them. He brushed against her in the crowds and once he took her arm to get her attention to point out something. Their mood grew playful and she relaxed more than she had in weeks. He teased her. She teased him back. Their hands brushed, and for a quick second she thought he was going to take her hand in his.

And that would have been fine with her.

They continued down the rows of tents and booths until she came to one filled with watercolor paintings. "Look, it's the beach at sunrise." She pointed to a beautiful painting with shades of pinks flowing above the splashing waves on the beach.

"Still a sunrise person, I see." Will smiled.

"I do love the sunrise. My favorite time of the day. It's like a blank slate and you can write whatever you want on it." Ashley's heart and mind filled with memories. The sunrises they watched together. The quiet moments they sat and watched the sun burst above the horizon. Sitting on the cool sand, holding hands.

"I remember, Ash. I remember everything." Will's voice was low, and he looked at her with such an expression of longing mixed in with hurt.

"I wish…" Ashley paused, uncertain if she should go on. "I wish things had been different, that things had ended differently, that we had at the very least stayed friends. I missed our friendship."

"You dumped me, Ash." Wills voice was still low, filled with reproach and a hint of pain.

And just like that the comfortable ease that had surrounded them vanished on the sea breeze.

"I…" She felt her cheeks flush. "I did. I know that. I handled the whole thing badly. I just thought we wanted different things from life."

* * * * *

No, he'd wanted what she wanted, but he'd had responsibilities that she didn't have. He had to take care of Whitney. He would have loved to have the luxury of earning money for college instead of putting food on the table. He would have loved to have more time to study to make better grades instead of a constant stream of any job he could find just to keep Whitney with him, fed, and dressed in the very occasional new clothes. He would have loved to have finished high school, instead of getting his GED years later.

But then, Ashley wouldn't have known that, because there was no way was he going to let anyone know that Warren had disappeared. Warren was gone so long that time Will had to drop out of high school and take two jobs. He and Whitney had kept the secret, always afraid someone would find out and take Whitney away. He'd been eighteen then, but he'd known there was slim to no chance that child services would have let him keep Whitney with him. Warren had been gone a month and then had shown up with one hundred dollars to his name. He'd stayed a few weeks, then was gone again.

The weeks had blurred that last year when Ashley had still been going to high school—and he should have too —but he'd been busy working. They'd never known when Warren would show up or leave. Whitney had taken to loudly calling out "Bye, Dad" whenever she saw a neighbor nearby as she left the apartment. Not that Warren was there often to hear it.

Will still could remember the afternoon when Whitney, clutching a twenty dollar bill, had looked at him with fear in her eyes. "This is all we have and Dad hasn't been back for a really long time." Tears had trailed down her cheeks. "What if they take me away from you? You won't let that happen, will you?"

He'd sat down next to her and put his arm around his sister's shoulders. "I won't let that happen."

"Promise you won't tell anyone that Dad is gone. Promise me."

"I won't tell anyone. I promise."

Whitney had looked a little relieved then, but she was old enough to know that twenty dollars wasn't going to get them very far.

He'd quit high school the next day and took a second

job. He made enough to pay their meager rent on the dive they lived in, and put food on the table. Occasionally Warren would show up with a bit of money. Sometimes he stayed for months at a time, and Whitney would get her hopes up, only to have them dashed again and again.

Will pushed the memories aside. He couldn't change the past, and he hadn't been able to tell Ashley what had been going on back then. He and Whitney had sworn to keep the secret between the two of them, and he'd kept his promise to his sister all these years. He wasn't going to break it, even now.

"We should go find that snow cone for Mia." Ashley's voice tugged him from his thoughts, brought him back to the present.

"We should." They turned to head to the food trucks when Lucille showed up right in front of them.

"Well, hello there Will, Ashley." Lucille stood blocking their path, or their escape, depending on how he looked at it. He noticed that Lucille, too, had on heels at the festival. Sometimes women and their choice of clothing confounded him.

"Miss Sanderson." Ashley smiled at the woman.

"I just saw Will's father playing cards with Victoria's daughter at the gazebo. Little Mia looks a little peaked, but then we did need Victoria to run the baking contest. She's the chairwoman of the event this year, of course. She is every year. So, of course she was needed there."

"Of course." Will wondered if Lucille would notice the sarcasm in his voice. *Of course* a baking contest was more important than a child.

"Victoria is the president of the Ashland Belle Society this year. We do a lot of good things for Indigo Bay, you know."

Will had no clue what the society did, but just nodded as if in agreement.

"I wouldn't mind joining and helping you." Ashley smiled at Lucille.

Lucille looked at her for a long moment. "Yes, well, most of the women in the society, well, their mamas and grandmothers have been in the society."

Will could see the hurt cloud Ashley's eyes. He stepped closer to her. "But I bet you'd love to have new people to help."

"Well, we'll see." Lucille answered without a hint of commitment.

"I'm sure you could all benefit from Ashley's enthusiasm. She loves Indigo Bay. She grew up here, you know."

"I do know."

Of course she knew. Lucille knew everything about everyone in Indigo Bay.

"Well, I better go back to the contest tent. They're about to announce the winner. I'm hoping it's not Miss Jenkins again. It would be the fourth year in a row. It's always her pies. The same year after year."

"So, you want some new blood in the baking contest winner list? Bet it would be good to do the same with that Belle Society." Will shot Lucille a pointed glance.

Lucille looked at him, then walked away without another word.

"Will, you didn't have to do that." Ashley turned to him. "I can take care of myself. I offered to join the society when I first got to town, but never heard back. I think they are firmly set in their ways. I'm just too... new... for them to want me in their group."

"That's just nonsense, Ash. They'd be lucky to have you."

"It's not your battle to fight."

"I was just trying to help."

"I know you were, but I've got to get the town to embrace me on my own terms, not thrust upon them where they don't want me."

"You're not that young girl from the crummy apartment on the wrong side of town anymore. You're a doctor, for Pete's sake." Will scrubbed a hand across his face.

"It's just going to take time for people to see me that way." Ashley turned and headed to the snow cone truck.

* * * * *

Will didn't know why Ashley was so focused on getting acceptance from the town. He, for one, didn't give a flip if anyone in this town liked him or not. But Ashley had always struggled to fit in, she'd craved it. He hoped she could win them over, but she ought to be proud of how far she'd come in life. And she'd created her success all on her own. He was pretty darn proud of her, even if she wasn't.

She was a doctor, what more did the town want from her?

They reached the food truck and purchased the treat for Mia. Will held the strawberry snow cone as they hurried back to the gazebo. Much to his surprise, Warren was still patiently sitting with Mia, teaching her a new card game. The little girl was listening intently and staring at the cards spread before her.

This was a side of Warren that Will had never seen. A patient man, taking time to explain a game to a child. That hadn't ever been the Warren who'd lived with them. Well, maybe it had been how it was before his mother died. But the Warren since Will's mother died had sure not been like that, and Will didn't have many memories before that, none that he'd admit he had. They all blurred into a swirl of nothingness.

"Here you go, Mia." Will held out the snow cone to the girl.

She reached for it. "Red, my favorite." She took a bit of the frozen ice. "Mr. Warren was teaching me how to play Old Maid."

"He was, was he?" Ashley sat on a bench next to the girl.

"Yep." The girl nodded and a bit of red ice dripped onto her dress. "Oh, no." Mia's eyes filled with tears.

"That's okay. Here, I'll see if I can get most of it off." Ashley wiped at the stain. "I'm sure it will wash out if your mom soaks it a bit. It's okay."

The girl didn't look convinced. She very carefully ate the rest of the cone. After she finished, she sat beside Ashley on the bench and leaned against her.

Will glanced at his watch. Vicki had been gone a long time and Mia was getting sleepy. He looked around but saw no sign of Vicki, so he settled into the chair beside Warren.

"Did you two have a nice time?" Warren looked at Will.

"We did. It's getting pretty crowded now, though."

"Did they have that big tent filled with tools?"

"How did you know about that?" Will eyed his father suspiciously.

"They have it every year at the festival. Lots of neat stuff."

"How many of these have you been to?"

"Quite a few."

Just how long had his father been back in Indigo Bay? Was he still flitting in and out of town when he went on his benders? Whitney hadn't been telling him everything about Warren, that's for sure. He made up his mind to talk to his sister later and get the whole truth.

He glanced over and saw Mia was sound asleep with

her head resting on Ashley's lap. He couldn't help but stare at Ashley's hand as she gentle stroked the tired girl's hair. He looked up and saw Vicki climb the steps to the gazebo and cross over to where they sat with Mia.

"That took a while." He couldn't help himself.

"I was in charge of the event. It had to go perfectly." Vicki dismissed his comment with a flick of her hand.

"She's napping? I'm never going to get her to go to sleep tonight if she's napped this afternoon."

"Vicki—er, Victoria—Mia's exhausted." Ashley looked up at the woman with a suggestion of disbelief in her eyes.

"She's a child. They get tired." Vicki glanced at her watch.

"She's just getting over being sick. She needs rest." Ashley said the reprimand in a patient but pointed tone.

"Ashley, do not tell me how to parent."

"I'm speaking as her doctor."

"Well, you aren't her doctor. Her doctor is in Charleston."

"I thought you brought Mia in to see Ashley." Will couldn't tolerate the way *Vicki* talked to Ashley like she was so much better than Ash.

"My mistake. It's not like she *did* anything for Mia."

Vicki walked over to where Mia was sleeping on Ashley. "Mia, get up. I'm going to take you home. I'll leave you with Cook, then I'll come back here and finish up my duties as the contest chairwoman."

The girl stirred and looked groggily up at her mother.

"Come on. I don't have much time. Get up." Vicki reached for the girl.

Mia sat up and got unsteadily to her feet.

"What is that?" Vicki pointed at the red stain on Mia's dress.

"I… I dropped my snow cone."

"That stain will never come out. Mia, you are so clumsy."

"I'm sorry Mommy."

"Mother, not Mommy. You're too old to be calling me Mommy."

Vicki turned to Ashley. "How could you let her get a stain like that on her new dress?"

The hair on the back of Will's neck stood up and he clinched his fist. He rose and stood face-to-face with Vicki. "I think what you meant to say is 'Thank you very much for watching Mia while I went off to pretend I was a big shot at the baking contest.'"

"Well… I never," Vicki sputtered. "Who do you think you are, talking to me like that?"

"Who do you think you are, talking to Ashley like that?"

"I should never have left her with people like you."

"People like us? People you don't think are as good as you?"

He felt Ashley's hand on his arm and he glanced at her. She tilted her head toward Mia, who stood motionless and wide-eyed. He immediately stopped his tirade. That was no way to talk in front of a kid.

Vicki, it seemed, had no compunction about answering his question in front of Mia though. "I meant people who are always causing trouble. People who pretend to be doctors but then send people away without doing anything for them. People who don't know how to mind their own business." Vicki grabbed Mia's hand. "Come on, we're leaving." She tugged her daughter across the gazebo platform. Mia turned when they got to the steps and gave a little wave, then they were gone.

Ashley looked up at Will. "You didn't need to defend me. I told you I can take care of myself."

"She just... got under my skin. She always has with her holier-than-thou attitude." He rubbed the back of his neck. "I shouldn't have said that stuff in front of Mia though."

"No, you shouldn't." Ashley took in a deep breath.

"She's wrong, you know." Warren put his hand on Ashley's arm. "You're a wonderful, caring doctor."

"Thank you. That means a lot." Ashley flashed Warren a small smile. She turned to look at Will. "You know, it's never a good idea to rile Vicki Holloway. There are always consequences."

"It's Victoria now, haven't you heard?" He grinned at Ashley, and she laughed.

Chapter Eight

Early Sunday morning Ashley slipped outside the cottage with a hot mug of coffee. She was determined to enjoy her morning ritual without being intimidated by the fact Will was staying right next door. She tugged a bright red wrap around her shoulders against the cool morning air. A flock of birds swooped through the air with a symphony of raucous calls, then it was back to simply the sounds of the crashing waves.

She glanced over and saw Will walk out on Whitney's deck. He looked over her direction and waved. Before she could stop herself, she jumped up and started to walk over towards him.

He met her halfway between the cottages. "Morning, Ash."

"Morning. Are you the only one up this early at Whitney's?"

"Whitney was exhausted last night. I think she overdid

it, but she never does listen to me. I'm hoping she sleeps in."

"It looked like Warren had a good time at the festival."

"I think he did."

A strained silence fell between them after the frivolous chit chat. She shifted her feet on the cool sand and watched the waves rolling to shore. The sun broke through the horizon and spilled its golden light on the ocean.

It was supposed to be the perfect spring day today, according to the app on her phone, sunny and mid-eighties. She planned to spend the day on the beach.

Before she had time to question her sanity, she turned to Will. "I'm going to have a beach day. You want to join me? I really need a day of just chilling."

"I'm not sure..." His eyes held a firm look of doubt.

"Sure, if you're busy. I just thought..."

"Well, if Whitney doesn't need me, I might join you."

"I'm going to make sandwiches and fruit salad, and I bought a pie at the festival yesterday." *Was she trying to tempt him with food? Was she that eager for him to say yes?*

"Well, if you're providing food, of course I'll join you." Will winked. "I could bring drinks. You still a sweet tea drinker?"

"I am."

"Well, I'll meet you out on the beach later this morning. I'm sure Whit can give me a few hours off." He smiled at her.

That smile of his. The one that managed to take her breath away and make her heart beat faster, even as she tried in vain to ignore it. Which was ridiculous because she was a grown woman now and she'd gotten over Will Layton years ago. Completely over him.

"I'll see you later, then." She turned and fled to the safety of her cottage.

* * * * *

Later that morning Will looked out the window and saw Ashley carting a beach wagon with a picnic basket, chairs, numerous tote bags, and a beach umbrella. Ashley never did do anything halfway. It appeared she was going to set up camp out there for the day, or the week, from the look of all the stuff she was hauling.

He grabbed the tea he'd made, draped a towel around his shoulders, and hurried out to the beach. "Planning on spending the week out here, Ash?"

She looked up from where she was struggling to dig out the beach blanket from the stack of items on the wagon. "What? Well, it was easier to load this up than keep running back to the cottage all day."

"Here, let me help." He reached for the blanket Ashley had finally freed from the wagon and let the breeze unfurl it. The blanket drifted to the sand and he tugged it a bit to straighten it. He reached for the umbrella and positioned it so there was shade and sun on the blanket, giving Ashley her choice of spots.

He still didn't know why he'd said yes to a beach day with Ashley. He should be working on Whitney's accounting, or helping her with... something. The last thing he should be doing was spending time with Ashley.

Yet, here he was.

Ashley had pulled her hair back in a braid and wore shorts and a tank top with a hint of a red bathing suit underneath, not that the water was really swimming weather yet. Her long, tanned legs stretched out from the modest shorts, and her feet were bare.

He should stop staring at her.

Yes, he should. *He could.*

He brought his attention back to unloading the beach wagon.

"Oh, I didn't bring glasses." He positioned the tea jug on the blanket.

"Got 'em." She opened the picnic basket that was perfectly packed with plates, silverware, glasses, and napkins, along with a generous amount of food. She pointed to a set of insulated tumblers. She swung the basket off the wagon and onto the blanket. "You want a chair?"

"Nah, I'm good with the blanket."

Ashley slid down and sat on the blanket in the sunny spot. He dropped beside her, partially in the sun, part in the shade. He stretched out and leaned back on his elbows. The beach was filling up with people enjoying the warm spring weather. A mother walked slowly along the water's edge with a young girl with blonde curls. The girl stopped and picked up a shell to drop in her bright red bucket. A pair of women passed, talking as they jogged along the sand. Just a normal sunny day at the beach, but he couldn't remember the last time he'd been to the beach. And he lived on an *island,* for crying out loud.

Only nothing at all felt normal to him this week. Not being back here in Indigo Bay. Not sitting within inches of Ashley.

"Ah, the sun feels so good." Ashley stretched like a cat.

He looked over at Ashley, who had her eyes closed and her face lifted to the sunshine. He could see the young Ashley hidden in the woman she'd become. Time wavered between the past and present.

* * * * *

The sun streamed over her like a warm blanket, heating her skin, soaking through until it felt like it was reaching all the way to her bones. She wasn't a winter person, not that winters were too bad here in South Carolina. She'd been working so hard for months. This was the first time she'd taken a day off from anything having to do with the clinic.

She slipped out of her tank top and shorts, revealing a modest, red, one-piece swimsuit with a retro look to it. She'd fallen in love with it when she saw it at a shop on Main Street. She settled back on the blanket and looked over at Will stretched out on the blanket, his eyes closed, soaking up the sun. He'd thrown an arm over his eyes and his breathing was slow and relaxed.

For a moment she floated between the past and the present. So many times they'd snuck away to the beach when they were kids and stolen moments together, best friends when they were younger, then boyfriend and girlfriend in high school.

Until... they weren't.

Will sat up and shrugged out of his t-shirt, grasping behind his neck and removing it with a smooth tug. His tanned skin glistened in the sunlight, and he settled back on the blanket.

Why was the man always insisting on being shirtless around her?

He'd filled out since their high school days. The boyish muscle had turned to firm, mature muscle in his arms, shoulders, and abs. He looked... good. Very good.

"You going to sit there and stare at me all day?" He opened one eye and grinned at her.

A blush heated her already sun-warmed face. "I... I wasn't staring."

"If you say so." He flashed an easy smile at her.

That smile was her undoing. All her defenses and rational thought escaped her. He wasn't right for her, she wasn't right for him. Nothing had changed.

And yet...

She wanted his friendship back, she wanted to enjoy this day in the sunshine with him.

"Ash."

"Hm?"

"You think too much."

* * * * *

Will knew Ashley was analyzing every little thing. It's what she did. Always. He'd bet anything that she was second-guessing her decision to invite him to the beach.

"It's just a picnic, Ash."

"I know."

"Then relax."

"I am relaxed." Ashley glared at him.

"Yes, I can see that." He shot her a grin.

"So when did you move back to town?" He figured he'd better change the subject.

"A year or so ago."

"All that education, a medical degree, and you came back here? Did you come back so you'd be close to your dad?"

"I…" Ashley's eyes clouded. "No, Dad died when I was in med school."

"Oh, Ash. I'm sorry. I didn't know."

"It was a heart attack. Sudden. I was away. I should have seen signs of heart problems though. But I was too busy. I rarely made it back home."

"I'm sure he understood. I'd think med school is crazy busy with impossible demands on your time."

"It is, but I should have made more of an effort. I always thought we'd have plenty of time together after I graduated." Ashley's face was etched in pain.

"I am sorry."

Ashley nodded.

"So then, why *did* you come back to Indigo Bay? There was nothing left here for you."

"It's my home. And—you'll think this is silly—I wanted to prove to the town that I've made something of myself, that they were wrong thinking I was just a poor little girl from the wrong side of town."

"You don't need to prove anything to them. Look at you. A successful doctor. Why anyone would come back to this town if they didn't have to, is beyond me."

"You just don't understand, Will."

"No, I don't."

Ashley sat and stared out at the waves, the light breeze teasing a few strands of hair loose from her braid. He watched her trail her fingers through the sand beside the blanket.

So much for him finding a safer topic. She must feel all alone in the world with no siblings, no parents, no grandparents. He at least had Whitney. Well, and Warren, but Will didn't really count him as family.

"So, I'm hungry." Will poked Ashley's arm to bring her out of her thoughts.

"Of course you are. You're always hungry." The corners of her mouth teased into a small smile.

"Well, let's have this feast." He sat up and handed the picnic basket to Ashley.

They sat and had their picnic while Ashley finally relaxed and regaled him with stories of her med-school days. He told her all about his home on Belle Island. The minutes rushed by into hours.

"Hey, you're getting a bit pink. You might want to put on some lotion." He pointed to Ashley's arms.

"I put some on, but I should probably put on more." She reached for the lotion and slathered it on her arms.

He watched, mesmerized when she began stroking it on her long legs, fascinated by each swipe she made as she spread the lotion on her skin.

"Here, I'll get your back." *Who was the traitor that just said that?*

"Uh, sure." She handed him the lotion.

He poured some lotion into his hand and moved to sit behind her. He rubbed it onto her warm skin, and his hands burned with memories etched deeply into his mind. His hands slid slowly over her shoulder, up her neck, then down her back. He worked the lotion in, hoping it would never absorb and he could keep trailing his hands over her.

"Do you have it?" He didn't miss the faint tremor in Ashley's voice.

"Ah. Yes, you're all good."

He reluctantly moved back over to his spot on the blanket and stretched out, concentrating on steadying his breath.

Ashley leaned back beside him again, inches from

him.

He let himself get lost in thoughts, and what-ifs, and the silken sunshine.

Later his thoughts, or maybe dreams, began to clear. His shoulder was numb, and he opened his eyes to find Ashley curled up asleep on his chest.

He didn't dare move, though the pins and needles begged him to, but his heart begged him not to. Not a muscle.

His traitorous shoulder twitched and Ashley stirred. She opened her eyes and smiled a lazy smile at him.

Then her eyes widened and she sat up straight. "Oh, sorry."

"No problem." He sat up and stretched his arm and shoulder.

"I guess the sun got to me."

"Nothing wrong with a little nap in the sunshine."

"I… I should probably go in. I've gotten a lot of sun."

"Or you could just move over here in the shade for a bit." But it *was* probably a good idea if she went inside, because if she moved over here next to him, he was pretty darn sure he would try to kiss her.

And he was pretty darn sure she'd let him.

But Ashley slowly rose, taking his hopes with her. "I'd better go."

Chapter Nine

It wasn't like Ashley to run late, but she was on Monday morning. She'd gotten sidetracked sitting and staring out at the ocean, thinking about yesterday with Will. Yesterday when she'd gotten up and fled from him like a scared little schoolgirl.

She'd wanted to nestle up next to him and spend the rest of the day in his arms. Talking, or silent, it didn't matter. But instead, she'd been her normal overly-cautious self and fled back to her cottage. He wasn't part of her plans. She had big goals and big dreams.

She pushed through the door to the clinic, expecting to see the waiting room full of people.

Not a one.

Jerri Lynn greeted her. "We've... um... had a few cancellations."

"Really? How many?"

"Well... most of your schedule for the day."

"Why? Did anyone give a reason?"

"No... but... I heard some talk."

Ashley crossed to the reception desk and eyed Jerri Lynn. "What talk?"

"Well, Victoria Tanner was saying that you didn't take care of her daughter properly when she brought her here. She's suggesting people go over to Charleston to the doctor she goes to over there."

"Mia had the virus that was going around. I told Vicki that. She needed to give it time to run its course."

"I know, poor kid. Though I did see Victoria brought Mia to the festival this weekend. She must have thought Mia was fine." Jerri Lynn shrugged.

Just then the phone rang and Jerri Lynn snatched it off the cradle. "Yes? Well, okay. I'll take you off today's schedule. Would you like to reschedule? Okay. Well, call when you're ready." Jerri Lynn hung up the phone.

"Another one?" Ashley sank into a chair in the waiting room. "Is anyone going to come in today?"

"I'm not sure. I'm sorry. Did you do something to make Victoria mad? She's not one to cross."

"You'd think I would have learned that lesson years ago, wouldn't you? Had a bit of a dustup at the festival, you know, after we watched Mia for her for hours." Ashley took a deep breath. Vicki—*Victoria* couldn't still have the power to ruin her and keep her tucked in the place Vicki thought she belonged, could she?

Ashley set her jaw, her teeth firmly clenched together.

She couldn't let this happen. Vicki had kept her out of the clubs she'd wanted to join in high school, kept her out of the Ashland Belle Society, though they rarely let anyone in it that wasn't at least a third generation Indigo Bay resident. Well, she *was* a third generation on her father's side—her family just hadn't run in the same circles as Vicki's. Goodness, they were hardly from the same *planet* as Vicki's.

But she was proud of her father. He'd been a hard worker. He'd done his best to raise Ashley on his own after her mother left. Her mother hadn't been able to handle being the outsider in Indigo Bay when she married her father. Indigo Bay was never going to accept her as a real resident. She'd left the town when Ashley was nine.

Ashley had grown up quickly then. She'd learned to get dinner on the table for when her father came home from work. She took their laundry to the basement in the apartment building and washed it in the coin laundry machines while she did her homework. Their neighbor Mrs. McCloud checked in on her and taught her to cook, so their dinners got better over the years.

Ashley had become a list maker to keep things running smoothly. She'd cleaned the tiny apartment, planned the weekly grocery list, and given it to her father to get the items.

She had a schedule. Mondays her father worked late, and she went to Mrs. McCloud's. Tuesdays she did laundry after school then made dinner for her dad. Wednesday was cleaning day. Thursdays she usually hung around the school until her father was ready to come home. On Friday nights they made dinner together and watched old black and white movies on their tiny TV.

Weekends were her time with her father. They'd go to the beach, or he'd take her into Charleston. Once a month he'd take her out to dinner. They'd get all dressed up and he'd let her pick a place to go. It was never an expensive place, but those nights were some of her dearest memories.

She'd liked their well-planned life and the control it gave her. Her father had laughed at her lists and her planner with everything written down, but he'd humored her. He'd been her biggest supporter and encouraged her to apply for scholarships for college and then medical school.

There was such a void in her life now that he was gone. She missed him every single minute. She wanted one more Friday night making dinner together with him. One more black and white movie night. One more hug...

Why all these memories had decided to surge over her and drown her right now was beyond her comprehension.

Her dad would have had the right thing to say to her today though, when she needed some support while the town, once again, dismissed her.

* * * * *

Will lounged in the open doorway to Coastal Creations, taking a break from the tedious work of sifting through all of Whitney's paperwork. He felt like he was finally making headway. He'd found the backup for the deductions she'd taken, along with some that she'd missed, and lectured her on keeping better track of expenses, though he knew it was a lost cause. He was going to find her a bookkeeper before he left town. She needed one to come in weekly and keep her on track, otherwise he was going to repeat this whole process again next year... and that would mean returning to Indigo Bay.

He looked up as Ashley came walking down the sidewalk towards him, lost in thought. The sunlight bounced off the reddish highlights in her hair. Her hair was pulled back in what he now considered her normal workday, out-of-the-way, practical braid.

Whitney had laughed at him when he'd mentioned it and said it was a French braid. Okay, was there a Spanish braid? An English braid? Women had strange terms for things, like the way they had fancy names for colors. Seafoam blue, chartreuse—he'd admit he had to look that one up. Or orange—why call it orange when you could call it tangerine, or melon, or coral? He watched Ashley come closer in her red dress. Red. Not a fancy what-the-heck-color dress.

"Hey, Ash. What are you doing wandering the streets

in the middle of the day?"

She looked up, startled. "Oh, it's you. I... well, I have an unusually light schedule today."

"I thought doctors were always busy on Mondays, isn't that some kind of rule or something?"

"Well, I'm not." Her words came out in a short staccato burst.

"Hey, sorry. I didn't mean to make you mad." He reached out to touch her arm.

She sighed. "You didn't. I'm just... upset. Just about my entire day cancelled on me today."

"That's strange."

"Not so strange when I heard Vicki's been spreading rumors about me. How I didn't take care of Mia and who knows what else."

Will felt a lump in his throat. He'd caused this by telling Vicki off at the festival, and Vicki had gotten even by taking it out on Ashley.

"I'm so sorry, Ash. It's my fault. I stood up to her and told her off. You said it wasn't good to make Vicki mad. I should have listened to you. I'm sorry."

"It's not your fault. She was already gunning for me. I'm sure she's behind me not getting into the Ashland Belle Society, too. She's never liked me."

"Vicki only likes herself. You saw how she treated Mia."

"Well, people in Indigo Bay listen to her." Ashley shaded her eyes with her hand and looked down the street. "I told Jerri Lynn to call if anyone else shows up at the clinic. I'm headed to Sweet Caroline's to drown my sorrows in a piece of her pecan pie and some sweet tea."

"How about I join you?"

"If you want."

"Ouch, don't sound so enthusiastic." He grabbed at his heart with an exaggerated grimace.

She sent him a wry smile. "I'm sorry. Let me try that again. I'd love to have the company. I just hope I don't clear out Sweet Caroline's when I go in there."

"More pie for us, then. Let's go." He placed his hand on her elbow, steering her down the street. "Caroline's pecan pie always cheers you up."

"I'm afraid it might take more than pie to fix things this time."

* * * * *

Will held the door open for Ashley as they entered the cafe. It took a moment for her eyes to adjust from the bright sunshine to the darker interior of the restaurant. Caroline hurried up to them.

"Will, I was hoping you'd come back here again before you left town. Ashley, always good to see you."

Unless, of course, her being here drove away Caroline's customers...

Caroline led them to a table by the window and they slipped into their seats.

"We'll have two pecan pie slices and two teas." Will ordered for both of them.

"Coming right up."

Ashley looked around the restaurant and caught the furtive glances some of the customers were throwing their way. "From the looks of it, most of the people here have heard Vicki's rumors."

"Or maybe they are wondering why a beautiful woman like you is here with a scoundrel like me." Will teased her in an obvious attempt to make her smile. "Or maybe some of them are remembering we were an item back in the day."

"Or they heard Vicki's talk…" Ashley wasn't going to let Will coax a smile out of her. If Vicki continued, she might ruin Ashley's attempt at expanding the clinic. It probably wasn't what Doc Browning had planned when he hired Ashley to run the clinic while he was on leave. She'd hoped he'd keep her on after he returned, but how could he if the town avoided the clinic if she was there? What if she ruined his practice before he came back?

Let the pity party begin.

She wasn't usually like this. She was upbeat and worked her plan and things fell into place.

She just hadn't taken Vicki Holloway—*Victoria Tanner* —into her plans.

Caroline brought their pie and drinks. "Here you go. I don't usually see you in here in the middle of the afternoon, Ashley."

"Well, I'm not very busy today."

Caroline's eyes were full of sympathy. "I heard the talk.

Sorry about that. Vicki can be difficult at times."

"It's Victoria, now, haven't you heard?" Will grinned.

"She'll always be Vicki to me." Caroline put her hand on Ashley's shoulder. "Don't you worry. This will blow over."

Ashley wanted to believe Caroline, but she just wasn't sure.

* * * * *

Will looked over at Ashley as she half-heartedly ate her pecan pie. He'd like to tell Vicki exactly what he thought of her and her mean-spirited rumor mill. But since he'd been the one to upset Vicki in the first place, he didn't think calling her out on her rumors would help the situation. He needed to figure out a way to fix things though. He couldn't stand to see the hurt look on Ashley's face.

She glanced up at him and caught him staring at her.

"I'll be okay, Will. Don't worry about me."

"I know you'll be okay. You always are." He reached across the table and took her hand. "Caroline's right. This will blow over. Things will go back to normal."

"I hope so for Doc Browning's sake."

Ashley's phone rang and she snatched her hand back. She dug out her phone. "It's Jerri Lynn." She tapped the screen and answered the call. "Okay. Yes. Okay, I'll be right there."

Ashley put the phone back in her purse. "I've got to go. I actually had an emergency come in."

"Go on, I'll get this."

"Thanks, and Will?"

"Yes?"

"Thanks for coming with me and trying to cheer me up."

"Any time."

He watched Ashley hurry out of the restaurant and went back to eating his pecan pie. And the last half of Ashley's. No use letting a good piece of pie go to waste.

Caroline came over and slipped into Ashley's vacated seat. "So... you and Ashley?"

"There is no me and Ashley. I was just trying to cheer her up a bit."

"If you say so."

"I *do* say so." He set his glass down on the table with an emphatic that-is-that.

"Can I just say one more thing?" Caroline look directly at him.

"Can I stop you?"

"Probably not." Caroline smiled. "I can see the way you look at her. Maybe it's time you gave yourself a second chance with her."

"Ashley doesn't want a second chance with me. She has her plans and she never varies from them. Everyone knows that. She plans so she can control her world... though this Vicki thing is putting her in a spin." He leaned forward. "Anyway, I'm leaving pretty soon."

"Maybe there's a reason you came back to Indigo Bay

right now. Maybe it's to give yourself a second chance with Ashley. Maybe it's to give yourself a chance to make peace with your father. Sometimes the universe gives you what you need whether you know you need it or not."

Will fiddled with the spoon in front of him. "I think it was all a coincidence. Well, Whitney didn't tell me that Warren was here, or I never would have come."

"Yes, you would have. You'll always come when Whitney needs you." Caroline contradicted his protest.

He sighed. "I can never say no to Whit. You're right there."

"Maybe it's time you make peace with *all* your past, Will. As we grow older we sort out our past. Make peace with what we can. People change, you know. Maybe you need to give them a chance. Forgive people and move on." She reached over and settled his hand that was still fidgeting with the spoon. "Maybe it's time for you to do that."

Caroline got up without another word, and walked away to wait on some new customers entering Sweet Caroline's. He took the last sip of his tea.

Maybe Caroline was right. Maybe it was time to grow up and make peace with his past. The problem? He'd no clue how to do that.

Chapter Ten

Will barbecued burgers for dinner, then Whit had insisted on washing the dishes and Warren had gone in to watch a baseball game on TV. Will wandered out on the beach to catch the reflections of the sunset. He strolled aimlessly down the beach with his mind in a whirl of memories from the past and feelings from the last week.

His father was not at all what he expected, though Will still half expected him to just up and leave as soon as he was recovered enough to get around on his own. It's what Warren did best... disappear.

Then there was the whole Ashley thing. Even though she'd broken his heart and he knew better than to trust her, he was still drawn to her. She had an irresistible pull that tugged at him and made him forget his resolve to stay unattached to anyone who might leave him again. Ashley definitely fit that bill.

As if the universe were laughing at him, he glanced up to see Ashley slowly walking towards him, seemingly conjured up from his thoughts. She lifted a hand in a small wave as she approached.

"Looks like we had the same idea. It's such a lovely evening. The weather has been perfect this week, hasn't it?"

Sure, he could talk about the weather with the best of them. He turned back toward the way he'd come and fell into step beside her. "Yep, nice weather."

Why would they talk about something important or meaningful... like the fact that the sunset was throwing rays of color across the delicate curves of her cheeks, or the fact that her lips were the tiniest bit moist and he longed to lean over and kiss them?

"Supposed to heat up soon." He meant the weather, not the air between them that crackled with electricity. Surely she felt it too?

"I heard that. Getting much warmer next week. Spring is always such a roller coaster here in Indigo Bay."

"Ash." He reached out a hand and stopped her, knowing he was making a mistake. A really big mistake.

She turned slowly to face him.

"I swear, if I don't kiss you within the next ten seconds..." He leaned forward and pressed a questioning kiss against her soft lips.

She slipped a hand onto his shoulder and stepped closer. He wrapped an arm around her and deepened the kiss. A kiss filled with years-long urgency. A kiss he'd thought would never happen again.

She finally pulled back and looked directly into his eyes. "I... I'm not sure that was very smart..."

"Probably not." He shrugged and pulled her close to him, holding her wrapped in his arms. It probably wasn't the brightest idea he'd ever had, but he wanted to kiss her again.

She rested her head against his shoulder, and they stood looking out at the sea. A peace settled over him, one he hadn't felt in years. Ashley had this way of making him feel like he was right where he was supposed to be.

* * * * *

Ashley could feel Will's heart pounding as she leaned against his chest. Their hearts beat in sync, drawing them closer.

Closer to danger.

Because Will Layton was not part of her carefully mapped-out plans.

He gently reached over and tilted her face to his. She sank into another one of his delicious kisses. She could remember every nuance of his lips, of his touch.

This time he pulled back and looked at her. "I've missed you, Ash. Missed these kisses. Missed our friendship."

She looked at the golden rays of sunset illuminating every angle of his face, the one that had haunted her dreams for years. "I've missed you, too."

This day was not turning out like she'd planned, from the sudden lack of patients to the kiss that stirred up feelings she'd spent years burying deep from conscious thought.

Will traced a finger along her cheek, leaving a burning trail of memories in its wake. Her world started spinning out of control, a feeling she hated with every fiber of her being. Never, ever, would she let circumstances or anyone control her life. Not anymore.

She took a tentative step backwards. Then another one, more determined this time. "Will, we can't do this."

"Why not?"

"Because… well, because."

"That's a valid reason." He cocked his head to one side and watched her every move. He reached out a hand and slowly encircled her wrist, pulling her gently back to him.

She didn't even try to resist. She fell into his arms and his kisses rained down on her. She'd give into the kisses now, and sort out rational thought later. That was a plan she could deal with.

* * * * *

Ashley sat on the edge of her bed, slowly unbraiding her hair. The light from the lamp on her nightstand spilled across the silky softness of the comforter. She reached a hand up and touched her lips. She could still feel the heat of his kisses, feel the way her heart had flip-flopped when Will held her. She could feel the way he'd kissed her one last time when he walked her back to her cottage and she'd watched him saunter away in the moonlight.

What was she thinking? He wasn't part of her life now. He lived three states away, bartending, still floating through life.

She had plans.

She had goals.

And her life marched in rigid step with those goals.

She rose from the bed and crossed over to the window. With a tug, she threw open the window and let the sea breeze rush in, soothing her jangled nerves. The tangy scent washed over her. Every inch of her skin felt alive tonight.

Will had always been able to do this to her, throw her off-center and make her question herself. He'd always tried to encourage her to do spontaneous things. Like years ago there was that time they'd jumped into the ocean at midnight under the full moon, fully clothed, swimming and splashing and laughing. The heady feeling of freedom had washed over her as they'd frolicked in the waves. It had been one of the best nights of her life, and she remembered every little detail of it.

But one week later there'd no longer been a Will and Ashley.

She'd broken up with him in her anger over him dropping out of high school. *Who did that?* A person needed a high school education and college or at least some kind of training to get on in this world, to be a success.

She stared out the window at the waves shimmering in the moonlight. Though, to be honest, she'd followed her careful plans and returned to Indigo Bay intent on proving to the people in town she was more than that girl from the wrong side of town. And look where that had gotten her...

Vicki had crushed her dreams with a few well-placed rumors.

She crossed to her bed and flopped down on the comforter, sprawling her arms wide, staring up at the lazy blades of the slowly revolving ceiling fan. It spun in circles, just like her life was doing these days.

Chapter Eleven

Ashley awoke the next morning still sprawled on her bed in her clothes and twisted in the covers. She scrubbed her hand over her face, chasing away the last vestige of sleep. A bit of light slipped through the open window. She sat up and stretched her arms.

The pity party of yesterday was over.

She pushed off the bed and glanced out at the beginning of the sunrise. A new day, a new beginning. A new day was as wondrous to her as turning the page to a new day in her planner. A blank page, ready to be filled with steps towards her goals.

Vicki couldn't ruin her hard won status in this town. Ashley wouldn't let her. She walked over to the dresser, her mind whirling with thoughts, grabbed her planner, and started jotting down ideas. Somehow, some way, she was going to expand the clinic's business before Doc Browning returned, and she was going to get him to ask her to stay on. Then everyone in Indigo Bay would see that she'd made a success of her life and know she was a competent doctor.

She might even convince the Ashford Belles to let her join in their exclusive club.

Today was going to be a great day.

* * * * *

Today was starting out as a lousy one.

Will swiped at the stream of spilled orange juice from the glass that had slipped from Warren's hand.

"I'm sorry about that." Warren sat at the table, mopping up the spill on the tabletop while Will knelt on the floor. Where was Whitney this morning? It was her idea for Warren to be here so she could help him...

"Not your fault. I should have made sure you had a grip on it before I let go." Will picked up the pieces of broken glass.

He was always picking up the pieces here in Indigo Bay.

He was annoyed he'd overslept this morning and missed any chance to see Ashley before she left for work, but it was no wonder he'd slept in. He'd spent most of the night tossing and turning, wavering between being thrilled he'd connected with Ashley again and reliving every moment of every kiss last night, and chastising himself, wondering what the heck he was doing. Hadn't he sworn off women, especially women who'd proven they leave him?

You'd think he would have learned his lesson by now. If you let people get too close to you, if you cared about them… they would eventually leave you, one way or the other. Like his mother had. Like his father had. Like Ashley had.

Why would he set himself up for that again?

He wouldn't.

Last night was a mistake. It was the last time he'd kiss Ashley. It was. He turned around in determination to see Whitney standing there watching him.

"You were out late last night, Willie." Whitney cocked her head to one side.

"Didn't know I had a curfew."

"You don't." His sister lounged against the counter. "So, I also noticed Whitney's light come on right after I heard you come inside. Were you two out together?"

"I don't owe you explanations on my comings and goings, Whit."

"Ah, I thought so." Whitney grinned. "I knew you two would reconnect. You're perfect for each other."

"As seen by the fact that we broke up and never saw each other again for years." Surely Whitney wouldn't miss the sarcasm…

"Minor misstep on your way to happiness. Trust me."

"Sure, I trust you. Because you always tell me the truth. The whole truth. No details left out." He pinned her with a glare and nodded his head towards Warren.

"I tell you what you need to know." Whit grinned

again then shrugged.

"No, you tell me what you *want* me to know."

"That, too." His sister reached into the cabinet for a coffee mug. "Because I usually know better than you, brother dear, what's good for you."

"You don't say." He scowled, unwilling to share the details of his night with Ashley, mainly because he wasn't sure himself how he felt about last night. Yes he did. It wasn't going to happen again. Ever.

"I *do* say. I'm your biggest fan, Willie. You know that. I just want… I want you to be happy."

"I'm the happiest darn man alive, sis." Will whirled around and slammed out of the cottage.

* * * * *

Will pushed through the door of Sweet Caroline's. In the hurry to leave Whitney's house, he realized he hadn't bothered to fix himself something to eat for breakfast. One of Caroline's cinnamon rolls and a big mug of coffee should turn his morning around.

Or not.

He stared at the familiar fancy braid across the room. Ashley had her back to him, but he recognized the set of her shoulders. She was scribbling furiously in her planner. Always her planner. He didn't think he was ready to face her so soon.

What if?

What if, what?

What if she smiled at him and leaned up for him to kiss

her? Would he kiss her? What if she got up and ran out? What if she didn't feel the same way he did about last night? How the heck did he feel about last night?

Caroline walked up to him and tilted her head towards Ashely. "Ashley's sitting by the window, you should go sit with her."

"I think I'll go eat elsewhere." He needed more time to sort things out. Lots more time... *like how many more days was he supposed to be here in Indigo Bay?*

"You know you want a cinnamon roll."

"I think I'm not hungry now."

"Never knew you for a coward." Caroline swished at him with the dish towel she had in her hand. "Go on. Sit with her."

Caroline was just like Whitney. Both of them always got their way. Always. It was a manner they had about them. People just seemed to do what they asked.

Will sighed. "Okay, I'm going over there. But I'm just stating for the record that I don't think it's a very good idea."

He crossed over to where Whitney had her head bowed over her planner, her pen busily writing in the swirling penmanship of perfectly formed letters.

"Hey, Ash."

She looked up and smiled at him, then the smile slipped from her face as if she'd deliberately taken it and hidden it away. "Morning."

"Mind if I join you?"

119

She paused, then gave a little nod.

He slipped into the chair across from her, though he wanted to sit in the chair right beside her, but he was unsure of—well, everything. He reached for the menu on the table, not that he needed it, as he knew everything on it. Not much had changed over the years at Sweet Caroline's, which was strangely comforting this morning. A waitress came over and he ordered a cinnamon roll and coffee while Ashley sat without saying a word.

He looked out the window at the people strolling by. Townspeople heading to work. Tourists out enjoying the early morning sunshine. No one rushing. No one as confused as he was...

"We should talk." Ashley interrupted his thoughts.

"About?" He knew darn well what they should talk about.

"Last night."

"You think it was a mistake, don't you?" He could see it in her eyes.

"I didn't say that."

He sat in stony silence and stared at her, waiting for the words he feared most.

"Will, I care about you. I always have. You were my first love, my best friend."

He crossed his arms and waited for the *but*...

"But we still want different things from life. I want to stay in Indigo Bay, and you've always made it clear that you can't stand the town and can't wait to leave." She leaned forward. "But… but, I wish we could still stay friends. *Just* friends."

That seemed like the smart approach. Friends. Because that was about as much of his heart he was willing to give to this woman who'd had such a hold over him. She was right. The kisses last night had been a really big mistake. Really big.

And, of course, Ashley would be the one to call it quits.

"You're right. It's pointless to see if this goes anywhere. We've done that before. Besides, I'm going to be really busy wrapping things up for Whitney before it's time for me to leave." He almost believed his words.

"So we'll still be friends?"

"Sure." He could be friends with her for a few days, right?

＊ ＊ ＊ ＊ ＊

Will left Sweet Caroline's after an awkward breakfast with Ashley. He'd agreed they should just be friends, so why did her suggestion… sting? It was the sensible thing to do. Besides, maybe he wouldn't even see Ashley again before he left town.

That thought caused a momentary panic to race through him, which he promptly stomped down. He didn't care if he saw her again or not. It would probably be best if he *didn't* see her again.

Probably.

He headed back to Whitney's shop, strolling slowly down the sidewalk in the warm spring sunshine. He passed by Happy Paws Pet Shop and Lucille Sanderson hurried out with a little white fluffy dog in her arms. He glanced in each direction and saw there was no escape, so he pasted on a welcoming smile.

"Miss Sanderson."

"Will, there you are. I was going to stop by Whitney's shop and talk to you. I wondered if you could do me a big favor."

Will eyed her suspiciously. What in the world could *he* do to help Lucille Sanderson? "What is it?"

"Well, my great-niece, Maggie, is in town from Georgia. I thought that maybe you could take her out? Show her around? She's such a sweet girl."

Will pictured a younger, carbon copy of Lucille and his mind started racing, looking for an excuse. "I'm pretty busy helping out Whitney."

"Surely you could find time."

"I have to help out with Warren, too."

"No time at all?" Lucille threw him an I-don't-believe-you look.

"I'd love to but I… uh… kind of have a girlfriend."

"You do?" Lucille looked at him doubtfully.

"Yes." His mind scrambled for an excuse she'd take. "I… I'm seeing Ashley Harden."

"Well, you don't say. You two were an item back in the day, weren't you? Well, I wouldn't want you to cheat on her, of course not. You and Ashley. You don't say."

He couldn't believe he *did* say.

"Well, then. I'll have to find someone else to show Maggie around. I'm sure I'll find someone. She's a lovely girl." Lucille put her fluffy pup down on the sidewalk. The dog had a pink, jewel-studded collar. Lucille's high heels matched the pink in the dog's collar exactly. "Come along, Princess."

Princess. Will hid a smile. He shook his head as he watched Lucille head down the sidewalk.

Will sighed and ran his knuckles along his chin. What had he done? He wished he could take back his excuse. He could have said he had a girlfriend back home. Why in the world had he said he was dating Ashley? Lucille was sure to spread the news all over town that he and Ashley were back together.

Only they weren't.

Chapter Twelve

Ashley poked her head into Whitney's shop on her way home from work, a workday where she'd seen exactly three patients. She wanted one last look at Whitney's hand and figured a house call—or place-of-business call—was the easiest way to accomplish that. It wasn't that she was hoping to see Will.

It wasn't.

No one was in the front room of Coastal Creations when she entered. Ashley browsed around looking at some of the jewelry displays thinking Whitney would come out from the backroom at any moment. Finally she decided to call out. "Whitney? You here?"

Will came walking out of the back room. His navy blue t-shirt fit his frame like a second skin. His worn jeans covered his long legs and he had on his inevitable sandals. She swore he'd even worn them in the dead of winter, such as winter was in Indigo Bay.

"Ash. Sorry, I didn't hear you come in."

"I... uh... I was looking for Whitney. Thought I'd check her hand one last time."

"She left to go home already." He lounged against the doorframe.

"Oh."

"You could probably catch her there."

"Yes, I should do that."

"I told her I'd lock up the shop when I finished up."

Ashley stood for a moment as the awkwardness swirled around them. "I was looking at her jewelry. She has some fabulous pieces, doesn't she? She's so talented."

"That she is." Will hadn't budged from the position he'd taken, barely a step into the front showroom.

"Well, I'll go check on her at the cottage."

Will nodded without saying a word.

She turned and fled out onto the sidewalk, anything to get away from the uneasy atmosphere in the shop.

She was reasonably confident she and Will were going to be a flop at this let's-just-be-friends thing.

* * * * *

Will waited until he was sure Ashley would have had plenty of time to check out Whitney's hand before he headed back to his sister's cottage. He didn't want to run into Ashley again. Two times in one day had been his limit.

He strolled along the streets in the evening light, wandering his way back to the cottage. A breeze picked up with the faint scent of an approaching storm. That was fine with him. He wouldn't mind sitting by Whit's large picture window and watching a storm come in. Some thunder and lightning suited his mood just fine.

He climbed the stairs and entered the cottage.

"We're back here." Whitney called out.

He walked through the cottage and saw Warren sitting at the table. There was no sign of his wheelchair, but a walker sat near the wall. He must be getting better. Whitney stood by the stove putting the finishing touches on dinner. "I made roasted chicken and potatoes. There's a salad in the fridge. Dinner will be ready in a few minutes."

He walked to the refrigerator and pried open the door. He swiped a cold bottle of beer and popped off the top. He took a long swig of the cool, golden liquid.

Whitney looked at him. "You okay?"

"You betcha," he lied.

Whitney wrinkled her forehead. "Ashley seemed a bit off when she stopped by this evening. Did you guys argue?"

"Nothing to argue about." He took another sip of the beer.

"If you say so." Whitney shrugged. "Did you see Dad's using a walker now? He's getting stronger."

What did his sister want him to say? Warren's progress was not his concern.

Whitney glared at him and turned back to the stove.

He went to the cabinets and pulled out the dishes to set the table.

"Sit. I'll get the rest." Whitney motioned with a fork.

He sat at the table across from Warren, who was working on a crossword puzzle. "Five letter word for a fool."

"Sucker." *No, that's six.* "Chump." That was easy. Will shook his head.

Whitney put the rest of the meal on the table and slipped into the chair beside Warren. The three of them sat at the table, just like they should have so many years ago. Only then it had most often been only Will and Whitney.

"I missed a lot of these meals over the years. I'm sorry. I should have been there." Warren's eyes held a look of regret.

A shiver went through Will, like his father—no, *Warren*—could read his thoughts.

"I can't make it up to you two, and I can only offer my apology." Warren turned to Whit. "And I can't thank you enough for taking me in while I recover."

"Of course, Dad." Whitney smiled at him.

"It's more than I deserve."

"That's all in the past, Dad. I'm sure you did the best you could at the time."

"His best was to not be here for us?" Will couldn't help himself.

"I *am* sorry, son."

Will gritted his teeth at the word *son*.

"How many times are you going to make him say he's sorry, Willie?" Whit glared at him.

"A couple of meals together doesn't make us a family." Will stabbed a piece of chicken from the serving tray.

"You can be the most… stubborn… thickheaded… *chump*." Whitney waved her fork his direction. "Must be nice to be so righteous and never make a mistake."

"It's okay, Whitney. He's right. I was a lousy father."

Will finally agreed with something that was said at the table tonight.

He escaped to the beach as soon as dinner was finished.

"Don't worry about the mess. Really. I'll do the dishes…" Whit called after him as he firmly slid the door closed behind him. Her sarcastic tone of voice was not lost on him.

* * * * *

Ashley sat on the sand and watched the approaching storm. She should probably head back in before the lightning got any closer, but the luminous display over the ocean fascinated her. Brilliant flashes of light slashed through the gathering clouds and illuminated the whitecaps on the waves. She pulled her legs up close to her chest and wrapped her arms around them for warmth.

Just a few more minutes and she'd head in.

"You should go in before the storm hits."

She looked up to see Will. He dropped down to the sand beside her. "If we stay much longer, the rain is going to hit."

"I know. I love to watch the storms come in though." The electricity of the storm and the energy between them crackled around her.

It didn't help when he dropped an arm around her. "You cold?"

"A bit."

She ignored the warmth of his body next to her. "Did you have a nice dinner with Whitney and your father?"

"Whitney and *Warren*?" He corrected her.

"You know, you might want to try to get along with him. I'm not sure what your falling out was, but he's your father. You're lucky to have him."

"Lucky. Right."

She whirled to face him. "You *are* lucky. I'd give anything to have my father back. I miss him. Every. Single. Day. You're throwing away the gift of family."

"Look, Ash. You don't know what you're talking about. I mean, I'm sorry about your father. Sorry you miss him so much. It must be nice to have had a great dad like you did. But that doesn't have anything to do with Warren and me."

"You're so pigheaded sometimes, Will. You get it in your mind that you're right and everyone else is wrong. There's no middle ground with you." She shrugged off his arm and pushed off the sand as drops of rain started pelting them. "Have you ever forgiven anyone for making a mistake? Do you just hold grudges forever?" Without missing a beat, the storm let loose and the rain started dumping on them, soaking her to the skin in moments.

Will jumped up. "Hurry." He grabbed her hand and started tugging her towards her cottage.

She wanted to yank her hand back, but instead left it in his warm grip and raced through the pouring rain to the safety of her home. They pushed through her door and stood dripping on the rug by the doorway.

She flipped on the light switch and nothing happened. "Electricity must be out. Stay there. I'll get some towels." She hurried down the dark hallway, felt around for towels in the linen closet, and returned to Will. "Here." She handed him a towel.

He took it, reached up, and roughly dried his hair. He shucked off his shirt and ran the towel over his bare skin. She could not quite see his hardened muscles in the low light but darn well knew they were there.

She turned away from him and wrapped the towel around her. "I'll be back." She fled to her room, fumbling in the dark, and slipped on dry clothes, a thick sweatshirt emblazoned with her med school, and comfortable yoga pants. With a deep breath, she squared her shoulders and headed back out to Will.

He stood in the big picture window, his silhouette framed with the almost constant flashes of lightning.

"Here, you must be cold." She dropped another towel

around his shoulders and handed him a large t-shirt she used as a sleep shirt.

He toweled dry and slipped the shirt on.

"Your jeans are sopping, but I can't help you there."

"Thanks." He turned to her, his voice low. "You know, both you and Whit said the same thing to me tonight."

"What's that?"

"That I'm stubborn and don't forgive easily."

"You are, and you don't." No use mincing words.

"Maybe I should try harder to make peace with Warren... and by try harder I mean try at all."

"I think you should. For Whitney's sake and for yours. You don't have to tell me what happened between you two, but whatever it was, it's been a long time. People change."

"I'm not sure I can believe Warren has changed."

"You could give him a chance. Take time to find out." She placed her hand on his arm and felt his muscle tighten under her touch. "People deserve second changes. We all make decisions that we regret later."

Right now she was regretting her firm decision to just be friends with Will because the urge to lean over and kiss him in the flashes of lightning and crashes of thunder was almost unbearable. A boom of thunder roared through the cottage and shook the walls. She jumped and bumped into Will, who reached out to steady her. His firm handhold seared her skin with memories of being in his arms.

"Ash? I think you and Whit are right. I should give Warren a chance." His voice was a low caress in the darkness.

"Good." She swallowed, ignoring the heat between them.

"And one other thing…"

"Hm?"

"I'm going to kiss you again." He turned to her and wrapped his arms around her. The water dripped off his jeans onto her bare feet and puddled around them. She wrapped her arms around his neck and held on. He leaned down and kissed her gently, then pulled away, a growly sigh escaping his lips.

That sigh was her undoing. She reached up on tiptoe and pulled his lips to hers.

Yep, she was certain she and Will were going to be a flop at the whole just friends thing.

* * * * *

Will stayed with Ashley as the storm crashed around them. They sat in front of the picture window and watched as the tempest faded away.

At least the one outside.

Inside? A hurricane of emotions swirled around them. He held her tucked against his side and couldn't help but think that she belonged there. He'd been surprised she'd let him kiss her again after her whole speech about being friends.

But the raw wildness of the storm had raged around

them, and he had wanted—no, needed—to kiss her. And he'd needed her to kiss him back. She had, with the same urgency that had surged through him.

They sat for hours and talked about everything and nothing. Finally the storm settled down to a gentle rain.

"I should probably go and let you get some sleep." He didn't loosen his hold on her.

"Probably should." She snuggled closer.

"The rain's let up enough for me to run back to Whit's without getting soaked again."

"Yes, it has."

"I don't want to leave." He pulled her closer.

"I… I don't want you to leave." Her voice sounded reluctant.

Was she reluctant for him to leave or reluctant that she wanted him to stay?

So they sat for another half an hour, not saying much, just holding each other.

He finally pulled away and stood. "I'm going to go now before… well, before… I don't." He reached down and tugged her to her feet. She followed him to the door and kissed him one last time.

He slipped out into the cool night air and headed back through the wet sand to Whit's cottage. A misty rain surrounded him as he slowly walked the distance. He turned back once and saw Ashley standing on her deck. She gave a small wave and went inside.

Loneliness wrapped around him, his arms heavy with

emptiness. He didn't know what they were doing, or where they were headed, but he knew he wanted to spend time and find out.

Even though it broke every rule he'd made for himself.

Even if it meant he had to forgive her for breaking his heart all those years ago.

He wanted to try again with her, he did. He couldn't be certain, when all was said and done, that she wouldn't leave him again, and he didn't think his heart could go through that again.

Chapter Thirteen

The next morning Will decided to have breakfast at Sweet Caroline's to avoid the whole family thing. He did think he'd take Ashley's advice and try talking to Warren. Maybe they could find some tentative common ground. Maybe the man had changed. Will needed a bit of time before he was ready to approach Warren.

He finished his meal and walked over to Coastal Creations. He pushed through the door and saw his sister standing by the display counter, a look of concern etched on her face. A uniformed man stood next to her taking notes on a pad of paper.

"Whit, what's going on?" He quickly crossed the room.

"I have two display cases of jewelry missing. They were here when I left yesterday." Whitney pointed to two empty displays.

The uniform man held out his hand. "Officer Moore."

"Nice to meet you, officer."

"I know I locked up when I left last night." Will thought back over leaving the shop. He was sure he'd checked the back door and locked the front door when he left.

"Were these pieces here when you left?" Whit motioned to the two empty displays.

"I honestly don't know, sis."

"Miss Layton said she left early yesterday. Did anyone come in after she left?" The officer looked at him, and Will had the slightest feeling he was being questioned as a suspect.

"No." He paused. "Well, just Ashley."

"Ashley?" The man scribbled a note.

"Ashley Harden."

"Was she alone in here?"

"No." Will paused. "Well, I was in the back and didn't hear her come in, so I don't know. But Ashley wouldn't have taken Whit's jewelry." Will looked at the man. "And, for the record, neither did I."

"He's right. Ashley's a friend. She didn't take these and of course Willie didn't." Whitney pointed to the displays.

"Um, hm." The man kept taking notes. "Well, there's no sign of forced entry that I can see."

"Ashley had nothing to do with this. You can put that in your notes." Will didn't think the man was listening.

"Have there been any other break-ins or thefts in town?" Whitney's forehead creased.

"None that have been reported." The officer closed his

notebook. "I'll do some checking around. I'll let you know if I come up with anything. And, ma'am? It's probably best if someone is always in the front room if the door is unlocked, or install a chime to ring in the back office if the front door is opened."

Nice. Talk to Whit like she's a child. He could see her bristle at the man's remark.

The officer left and Will turned to Whitney. "I'm sorry. I really didn't hear anyone else come in, but I was engrossed in numbers."

"It's not your fault. I should have just locked up when I left. I usually have a part-time worker here, but she called in sick. I also need to hire another one for the busy season this summer."

"Well, I know it wasn't Ashley that took your jewelry."

"I know it wasn't either." Whitney nodded. "I hope Officer Doubtful can track the missing pieces down. I already had them listed on the website and I have... *had*... an order for one of them."

* * * * *

In a change of pace, Ashley got to the clinic right when it was scheduled to open instead of an hour or so early. It's not like she had a lot of patients on the books. At last check she had one late-morning patient and a couple more in the afternoon. Anyway, she'd spent the morning in a hazy glow of dissecting every last minute she'd spent with Will last night. A smile spread across her face.

Jerri Lynn looked up from the reception desk. "Good,

you're here."

"What…" *Pull yourself together, woman.* "Why, did we get an emergency?"

"No… we have a problem."

"What's that?" Ashley crossed to the reception desk pushing all thoughts of Will behind her. Well, most of them. She concentrated on what Jerri Lynn was saying to her.

"I was doing some inventory this morning to see what drugs we might need to order. We have some missing…"

"Was the cabinet locked?"

"Yes, it was."

"That's strange. Then how could some be missing?" Ashley frowned.

"I was just getting ready to call the police, but thought I'd wait to make sure you hadn't moved them." Jerri Lynn reached for the phone.

"No, I didn't. I think it's a good idea to call the police."

A police officer arrived within minutes of the call. "I was right down the street. I'm Officer Moore. Dispatch said you had a theft?"

"We did." Ashley stepped forward and held out her hand. "Dr. Harden."

"Ashley Harden?" The officer looked at her with a hint of a frown.

"Yes." Ashley ignored the officer's strange look and pointed to the backroom. "There are some drugs missing from the locked cabinet. I don't know how that could happen."

"Who has access to the cabinet?"

"Just Jerri Lynn and me."

"Hm." The man jotted a note on a pad he carried. "Let's go see the backroom."

She led him to the room and gave him the list of missing drugs Jerri Lynn had carefully written down. He checked the back door. "This door kept locked?"

"Always."

"No sign of it being tampered with."

"So how did someone get in?" A frown creased Ashley's forehead.

"I'm not sure." The officer scribbled some more notes. "I'll check into things and get back to you." The man sent her another peculiar look.

"Thank you, officer."

The man left and Ashley sank into a chair in the waiting room. What else could go wrong? She'd chased away most of Doc Browning's patients and now there were missing drugs.

* * * * *

Will smiled when he saw Ashley ahead of him on the sidewalk as he strolled back to the cottage that evening. He hurried to catch up with her. "Hey, Ash."

Her eyes were tired and she gave him a weak smile. "Hi."

"Long day?"

"It was."

"So your patients started coming back?"

"No, actually two of my afternoon appointments cancelled. It's not that, though that does bother me. Jerri Lynn found some drugs missing from the locked cabinet." Ashley's eyes clouded.

"Really?" Will frowned. Two thefts in one day?

"Yes. I don't know how it could have happened. There's no sign of a break-in. I just don't understand."

"Get this. Someone stole jewelry from Whit's displays, too."

"Yesterday?"

"Yep."

"Did you call the police?"

"She did. An Officer Moore came out to check on things. He was kind of a jerk."

"He came to the clinic, too. He was giving me the strangest looks."

Will raked his hand through his hair. "Ah... well... he got it into his head that you were a suspect in Whit's break-in."

"How in the world did he get that idea?"

"He asked if anyone had been in the shop and I said you'd stopped by yesterday."

"Really? You think I took Whitney's jewelry?" Her words crackled with disbelief.

"No, of course not. That's not what I told him. I don't think you took anything and neither does Whit."

"Well, I bet Officer Moore does. He kept giving me a

look…"

"I don't care what he thinks, we know you didn't do it."

He and Ashley turned the corner and ran smack into Vicki Holloway. *Was he ever going to think of her as Victoria Tanner?*

Nope.

"Well, humph." Vicki huffed the words and took a step back. "I'm surprised to see you, Ashley."

Ashley frowned. "Why is that?"

"I thought by now you'd be down at the police station."

"What are you talking about *Vicki*?" Will moved closer to Ashley's side.

Vicki glared at him. "Well, Officer Moore was asking around town about Ashley today. Seeing if anything else had been stolen when Ashley was around. I heard there were drugs missing from the clinic and some of Whitney's jewelry was taken, too." Vicki's face was covered in an accusing glower, followed quickly by a triumphant smile.

"Knock it off, Vicki. Ashley didn't take anything." He glanced over to see a look of horror plastered on Ashley's face.

"Would you stop calling me Vicki? I go by Victoria now. Really, I don't think that's so much to ask."

"Okay, then, *Victoria*, Ashley didn't take anything. And you should quit spreading rumors around town."

"Officer Moore said she was his only lead."

"Officer Moore is an idiot and should try harder to do his job." Will's pulse pounded in his ears. Vicki was never going to change. She was always spreading rumors and distorting the truth. She *enjoyed* causing trouble for others. "Ashley had nothing to do with either of the thefts. Nothing."

"If you say so." Vicki shrugged, turned on her high heels, and stalked away from them.

* * * * *

Ashley clenched her fists as she watched Vicki walk away, her red heels clicking on the sidewalk. So Officer Moore thinks she's guilty of *both* of the robberies? No wonder more patients had cancelled this afternoon after Vicki had worked her magic spreading more rumors. Her face flushed with anger and she whirled toward Will. "Why did you tell Officer Moore I was there at Whitney's shop? Why didn't you defend me when he thought I was a suspect?"

"I *did* defend you."

"You didn't do a very good job of it, did you?"

"*I* didn't cause this mess. Anyway, you didn't do anything so it will all blow over soon."

"That's easy for you to say." She took another step away from him and held up her hand. "You're leaving in a few days. You don't have to stay here and face down the rumors Vicki's spreading. You don't have to tell Doc Browning that you've basically ruined his practice *and* there are missing drugs. You don't have to stay here and see how all the people in this town look at you with suspicion."

Will paused and gave her a long, searching look. "You know, Ash, you don't have to stay here and take that either."

"I'm not a quitter." She shot the words back at him.

"A quitter like me? That's what you mean?" His eyes flashed in anger now, too.

"No... I..."

"Never said you were a *quitter*, Ash. I'm just saying... you don't have to care what the town thinks of you. They aren't the judge and jury of your worth."

She swallowed. "Maybe not, but I've tried my whole life to get this town to see me as something other than the janitor's daughter. Now, it looks like I might end up in jail. It's going to prove their low opinion of me is right."

"No, you won't. They don't have any proof."

"They could still arrest me."

"Doubt it, but it wouldn't stick because I know you didn't do either of these."

"Everything, all I've worked to accomplish for so long, it's all ruined." Ashley didn't care if she sounded overly dramatic. She felt her life spinning out of her control and nothing she did seemed to stop the whirling.

Will reached out his hand and touched her arm. She jerked away. "Don't. You've done enough." She turned and hurried off down the sidewalk, putting as much distance between them as possible so he wouldn't have a chance to see the tears slipping down her face.

* * * * *

Will watched Ashley stumble down the street. He'd seen the beginning of tears in her eyes and knew she was hiding them from him.

But there it was, the beginning of her pulling away from him once again. And he couldn't erase the look he'd seen in her eyes when she'd insisted she wasn't a quitter. She still thought of him as one after all these years, because he'd dropped out of high school. That look would be ever etched in his mind.

Last night had been a mistake, one he couldn't afford to keep making. It didn't matter how sweet her kisses were or how great it had been to just sit and talk with her, the best friend he'd missed so much over the years.

None of that mattered now.

He'd forgotten what Ashley did best.

Leave him.

Chapter Fourteen

Will let the screen door slam behind him as he entered Whitney's house. One thing he'd decided though. He was going to talk to Warren and see if he could make peace with the man. For Whitney's sake.

"Warren? Where are you?"

The sound of silence was deafening. Will looked around. There was no crossword puzzle spread out on the table. No walker in the corner. He wandered back to the room where Warren had been staying. The bed was neatly made and the closet door partly closed. He slid it the rest of the way open and saw none of Warren's things hanging inside. He looked in the bathroom they all shared and Warren's shaving kit was missing.

The man was gone.

Which didn't surprise Will. Didn't surprise him one bit.

Everyone in his life was behaving true to form.

They were leaving him behind.

* * * * *

A beer and a bag of pretzels later he heard Whitney come home. Will sat on a chair on the deck, his back firmly in the direction of Ashley's cottage, in case she was cruel enough to come out and sit on her deck. He'd gotten outside first, so she should just skulk around in her cottage for all he cared.

Whit came walking out with a beer in her hand and dropped into a chair beside him. "Where's Dad?"

"Good question."

She stared at him. "What do you mean good question?"

Will took another swig from his beer. "There's no sign of him. He's gone. All his things are gone. He left. Vanished. You know, the thing he does best."

"Did you chase him off?" Whitney shot him an accusing look.

"He was gone when I got here."

His sister grabbed her cell phone from her pocket and tapped the screen, her forehead creased in worry. "He's not picking up."

"Oh so surprising."

"Quit being a jerk." She glared at him. "I'm going to leave a message for him to call."

"Do what you need to do. But he's gone."

"He probably just went back to his apartment."

"And decided not to answer your call?"

"Willie, you can be the most exasperating brother ever."

He probably could, but obviously he was a great judge of character, because the people around him were acting just like he knew they would.

"I'll call him back in a little bit."

"As you wish."

"No, I'm going to drive over there and make sure he's okay." Whitney stood.

"Whatever." Will took another sip of beer. "He's gone, Whit."

"He is not. He wouldn't leave again. He promised. I bet he just went back home. He's doing better. Did he leave a note?"

"Nope."

"Well, I'm going to go check on him."

Will sat and sipped his beer and finished off the pretzels. Not the most nutritious meal, but it suited him just fine. Luckily he hadn't made a fool of himself and tried to work things out with Warren and forgive him. A couple more days here to finish up things for Whit and he'd be gone... and he didn't plan on ever returning to Indigo Bay again.

* * * * *

Whit returned to the cottage about thirty minutes later. He could tell she'd been crying, but he knew better than to mention it.

"There's no sign of him at his apartment building and

he's not answering the door. The blinds are closed so I couldn't peek in. I should have gotten a key from him so I could check on him. What if he's hurt?"

"It's more likely he disappeared into a bottle again."

Whit looked at him, her eyes clouded with doubt. "I... I just don't think he'd do that again."

"He always does that, Whit. Just as soon as he seduces you into thinking he's going to stay. Poof. He's gone."

"Well, I don't believe it."

"Believe what you want, sis."

He got up from his chair. "You want to join me? I'm going in for another beer."

Whit nodded and dropped to a chair on the deck. He came back with two long-necked beers and a bag of trail mix. "Sorry, I finished the pretzels. Try these. Munch away."

Whitney took a handful of the mix and picked her way through it, eating one type at a time. First the candy-coated chocolate, then the pretzel sticks, then the dried fruit, then the nuts. He hid a smile. She'd eaten trail mix in that obsessive way since she was a young girl.

Will took a long sip of beer and settled back in his chair. "Been a heck of a day. You know, I'd just about decided to sit down with Warren and see if we could work things out. Try to find a way to at least... well, I don't know what I hoped for, but it doesn't really matter anymore."

"You were going to work things out with him?"

Whitney looked like she didn't believe him.

"I was going to try. I know it's been hard on you. But I don't trust him… and it appears I have good reason not to."

"Maybe he just went back to the apartment…"

"Without leaving you a note? I doubt that."

Whit leaned back in her chair and slowly nursed her beer. A look of defeat settled over her. He was sorry she was hurt again, but maybe this would finally convince her Warren will never change and she could quit getting her hopes up. He'd spent his whole life watching her get crushed every time their father disappeared. People don't change. It was silly to get your hopes up. It was crazy he'd gotten his hopes up about Ashley, too. He was no better off than his sister.

It was time to wipe the Indigo Bay sand from his feet and go home. Whitney could come to Belle Island and visit him, or they could meet somewhere, but he was done with this town. Done. Finished. Over it.

A couple more days and he'd be gone. He'd stay around just long enough to finish up Whitney's books and make sure she was okay with this whole Warren thing. As if a person ever got over their parent continually deserting them.

Chapter Fifteen

Ashley walked to the clinic the next morning, dreading hearing how many patients had cancelled today. She needed to call Doc Browning and tell him what was going on. She couldn't bear to ruin his practice. Maybe he could come back early or find someone else to work here until he could return. It wasn't fair to him for her to chase everyone away. Whether it was her fault or not, the town had decided she wasn't the doctor for them.

She opened the clinic door to find Lucille Sanderson and a young woman sitting in the waiting room.

"There you are, Ashley. I hope you don't mind. My niece, Maggie, isn't feeling well. It's probably that bug that's going around, but I'd feel better if you'd check her out."

Ashley looked at the young woman. She didn't look like she felt well at all. "No problem. I'll see her first thing."

"I have exam room one set up for you." Jerri Lynn motioned with a pen.

"Maggie, would you like to come this way with me?"

The young woman nodded and stood.

Lucille sat primly in the waiting room chair. "I'll be right here, Maggie."

"Thanks, Aunt Lucille."

Ashley took a brief medical history and examined Maggie. As Lucille had suspected, Ashley's best guess was Maggie had the virus that was doing its best to hit just about everyone in town.

"You'll feel better soon. Drink plenty of fluids and take it easy. You should feel better in a few days, but I'll warn you, this virus really seems to wipe people out. Expect to be tired for a few days afterward."

"Thanks for seeing me. I told Aunt Lucille it was probably the bug going around, but she insisted I come see you. She said it was better safe than sorry. I appreciate you fitting me in."

Ashley didn't want to admit there wasn't much fitting her in involved in seeing her, but didn't think it was smart to mention that.

She walked Maggie out to the waiting room. Lucille stood with a graceful swoop as only a southern-bred lady could pull off. "Is Maggie okay?"

"She'll be fine with some rest."

"I really appreciate you seeing us today. It was very kind of you." Lucille grabbed her pocketbook and headed to the reception desk. "I'll pay for Maggie's visit."

"I can pay for it, Aunt Lucille."

"Nonsense. You caught this nasty virus because you came to visit me." Lucille took out her checkbook.

"Call me if you have any problems or if you start to feel worse, okay?" Ashley turned to Maggie. The woman nodded.

"We'll be going now. Again, thank you for seeing us." Lucille took Maggie's arm and they walked to the door. Ashley followed them and stood in the doorway with the sunshine spilling in on the polished vinyl floor.

* * * * *

Whit had been moping around the cottage all morning, in between leaving messages on Warren's phone. A phone that was never answered.

"Look, Whit, you can stay here sulking all day, leaving message after message, but I'm headed to Coastal Creations to finish up the last of setting up your books. I have a bookkeeper coming by tomorrow to show her what I did, and you should be all set in the future. She's going to come weekly at first to keep you on track."

"I'm not sulking." Whit slammed the cabinet a bit too forcefully to prove her point.

"Okay, moping then."

Whit glared at him as he headed out the door.

Will took the long way to Whit's shop, not because it took him past the clinic, but because it was a beautiful, sunny morning. *That* was the reason. As he approached the clinic, he saw Lucille standing in the doorway with a young woman. Ashley stood in the entrance talking to them. Before he had a chance to do a quick getaway, Lucille looked up and waved at him. He took a deep breath and crossed the distance to the clinic.

"Will, this is my niece, Maggie."

The infamous Maggie. She wasn't a bit how he imagined, not that he was interested in taking her out. Or anyone out. "Nice to meet you, Maggie."

The woman nodded.

He stood awkwardly a few feet away from Ashley while Lucille sent him a strange look. He moved closer to Ashley… then Ashley sent a strange look. He pasted on a big smile and moved to lounge in the doorway right next to Ashley. He leaned over and whispered in her ear. "Go with me on this."

He pressed a quick kiss against Ashley's cheek and her eyes widened in surprise. "Morning, darlin'." He used his best southern drawl. "Missed you last night."

Ashley stared at him. "I…"

"I think it's wonderful that you and Will are seeing each other again." Lucille gracefully waved her hand their direction.

Ashley opened her mouth and before she had a chance to contradict Lucille, before he could even think clearly, he leaned over and kissed Ashley right on the lips. She must have forgotten she'd vowed she was done with him, because he would swear she kissed him back.

"I… ah…" Ashley pulled away, slowly, a bemused look on her face.

He thought she'd never looked more beautiful.

"I asked Will if he'd show Maggie around town." Lucille smiled. "But he told me how you two were dating again. That's nice."

"Aunt Lucille, I wish you'd quit trying to fix me up."

"I just want you to have a good time while you're here and spend some time with people your own age."

"I think you should probably get Maggie home now." Ashley still look a bit bewildered and took a small step away from him. He refrained from moving closer to her again, though he wanted to. He wanted to wrap his arms around her and kiss her again. Slowly. Thoroughly.

What was *wrong* with him? Ashley had made it clear there was nothing between them. Or had she? Her kiss just now hadn't been an I'm-done-with-you kiss.

Lucille nodded to Ashley. "I *should* get Maggie home. Thank you so much, Ashley." Lucille turned and led Maggie down the street toward her car.

Ashley whirled towards him. "What in the heck was that?"

Guess she'd gotten over that whole bemused, betwixt thing. "Sorry, Ash. She asked me to take out Maggie. I kept throwing excuses at why I couldn't, and finally I blurted out that we were dating…"

"Great, just great. What's the town going to think of me now? So now they think I'm dating you again, along with being a thief."

He looked at her and stepped back, his heart lurched in his chest. Why did he keep putting himself in this position? The one where Ashley could crush his heart. "And which one is worse? Being labeled a thief, or people assuming you're dating me?"

Her eyes widened. "No... I didn't mean... I mean... I'm sorry, that came out wrong. It's just... you kissed me and I wasn't expecting it."

"You kissed me back." He stood his ground. "But, I think you're right, Ash. We're just wrong for each other. Next time I see Miss Sanderson, I'll set her straight. Maybe I'll even take out her great-niece." Though he knew wouldn't take Maggie out. He was done with women.

He turned and walked away from Ashley without another word.

* * * * *

Ashley watched Will walk away, refusing to acknowledge the feelings he'd flamed when he pressed that kiss to her lips. Her heart was a traitor and she'd kissed him back, lost in the moment. So she'd taken her dismay about her reaction out on him.

She knew she'd hurt his feelings when she said that remark about what would the town think of her now, but he'd caught her off guard.

Did she care if the town thought they were going out again?

All she wanted was the town to see her as a successful doctor. Being tied to her high school boyfriend again would only make them see her as the girl she used to be. She'd tried so hard and come so far. She wasn't proud of herself and it sounded shallow, but dating someone whose ambition in life was being a bartender... well it didn't fit into her plans.

Yes, she was shallow.

No, she was practical.

Besides, she assuaged her guilt, Will didn't want to be in Indigo Bay and she did.

She turned to go back inside the clinic and put Will and his kisses behind her.

Ashley walked up to Jerri Lynn. "Well, that was unexpected... Miss Sanderson bringing Maggie here, I mean." Hopefully Jerri Lynn hadn't seen the whole kissing incident. *That* had been unexpected, too.

"Can't hurt anything to have the town see Miss Sanderson bring her niece in here," Jerri Lynn said thoughtfully.

Jerri Lynn was right. By afternoon the clinic waiting room was filled with patients again. Evidently Miss Sanderson's endorsement was stronger than Vicki—Victoria Tanner's—rumors. Ashley rushed around all afternoon seeing the much-needed patients. Maybe there was no need to call Doc Browning after all. She'd solved all her problems.

Well, except for the problem of the missing drugs, and

she was the one who was under suspicion. Oh, and the fact that the town now all thought she was dating Will Layton again.

* * * * *

Will wasn't sure if he or Whit was in the worse mood that night. They banged around the kitchen throwing dinner together, not saying much. Whit finally sank onto a chair, her eyes filled with tears. "I just... I just didn't think Dad would leave me again. I thought he'd changed."

Will went and knelt in front of his sister and took her hands in his. "I know you did. I'm sorry you got hurt."

"Willie, it's always going to be like this, isn't it? I'll take him back, he'll convince me it will be different... then he'll leave."

"I'm afraid so, sis."

A lone tear tracked down Whit's cheek. It broke his heart to see his father still have this hold over Whit. The man was worthless as a father.

"Promise me you won't let him fool you again." Will brushed a tear away from Whit's face.

"I won't. I think I finally learned my lesson. Though I did think he'd truly changed this time. He'd been visiting a lot the last few years and moved back here to live a while ago. Then, when he got hurt saving that little boy..."

"What little boy? What are you talking about?" Will sat

back on his heels.

Whit sighed. "He didn't want me to tell you about it. He wanted you to forgive him without knowing what he did. He wanted to be accepted for just... I don't know... for being himself, not because of anything he did."

"What *did* he do?"

"He was in Charleston one day picking up some supplies I needed for the shop, and a little boy darted into the street. A car was coming and Dad jumped into the street and knocked the little boy to safety. Dad got hit by the car though. I heard all about his bravery from the boy's mother. She was so grateful. It's been a rough recovery for him. With the alcohol problem, he didn't really want to get hooked on pain pills, so he's mainly just gutted through the pain since he got out of the hospital."

"I had no idea. I figured it was another drinking and driving accident..." Will was embarrassed that he hadn't even bothered to ask Warren how he'd gotten injured. Though, now that Warren had hurt Whit again, a bit of his guilt was lessened.

"Things had changed with him. Well, I thought so anyway." Whit got up and walked over to a small table by the window and grabbed a box of tissues. She snatched at one, and the box tumbled to the floor. She leaned down to pick it up, paused, and dropped to her knees. She reached under the couch then stood, her eyes wide, and held out an envelope. "It's Dad's handwriting."

That was different. Warren didn't usually leave a note, he just vanished. Will had no idea why Warren would change his ways now.

"It must have blown off the table and under the couch." She hurried back to her chair and ripped open the envelope.

Whitney,

There was a sudden opening in a rehab clinic in Savannah where I'm hoping to get some intense therapy to get back on my feet sooner. I got a ride from Bill from the church. I didn't want to bother you, you've already done so much for me.

This will give you and Will some time together without me interfering. I know he's still angry with me, and with good cause. You two just enjoy your last few days together and have fun. Give my best to Will and tell him I love him.

I'll call soon.

Love,

Dad

"He didn't just leave..." Tears poured down Whit's cheeks. "He went to rehab in Georgia to get stronger. I know Ashley had recommended that rehab place initially, but they hadn't had any room for him." Whit glanced at him with a fiercely protective look on her face. "I knew he wouldn't leave me again. I *knew* it."

Will stood and pulled a chair next to Whit. "I'm glad for you, Whit. Glad he didn't run off again."

Whit swiped at the tears on her face. "You think you could go see him before you leave? Try to work things out? Please? For me?"

"No." Will shook his head. "Not for you. But I *will* go for *me*. I don't make any promises, but I will go see him."

"Willie, you know when I said you were a stubborn, pigheaded chump?"

"I remember." He grinned at her.

"Well, you still are..." Whit smiled through her tears. "But you're the best brother in the whole world."

"You're not so bad as a little sister, either."

Chapter Sixteen

Ashley arrived at the clinic bright and early the next morning. The phone had rung non-stop yesterday, and Jerri Lynn had cheerfully filled the schedule. They already had a full day of patients on the books for today. She smiled as she entered the clinic, full of hope for a great, if busy, day.

She walked into the clinic and saw Officer Moore talking to Jerri Lynn. He turned when she entered. "There you are Dr. Harden."

"Officer, what can I do for you?" Ashley didn't really want to talk to the man after he'd gone around town basically accusing her of stealing from other businesses.

"Well… my boss wanted me to come let you know in person."

"Let me know what?" She stood facing the officer.

"Well… um… we caught the person involved in the robberies."

"Oh, you mean you're no longer going around town and asking other businesses if I've been in recently and if they are missing anything?"

"I was just doing my job, ma'am."

"Is that so?" Ashley felt her blood pressure rise. "So basically letting the town know I was your prime suspect without a bit of evidence was good police work?"

"I… I'm sorry about that. My boss gave me an earful about my conduct. I was over eager and wanted to make a name for myself by solving the case. I'm new here, and… well, I wanted people to accept me."

Ashley could relate to the fitting in part. "So, who was it?"

"It was a lady named Patricia Greene."

"She used to work for Doc Browning." Jerri Lynn's eyes widened. "He fired her."

"Well, she was here long enough to know to have a spare key to the clinic made, and she told us there's an extra key to the medicine cabinet in a hollowed out medical book on the Doc's bookshelf. She saw him get it one day."

Jerri Lynn looked surprised. "I've worked for him for years and didn't know he had one there."

"Well, she confessed it all."

"How did you catch her?" Ashley frowned.

"We caught her trying to fence some of Miss Layton's jewelry. Then she admitted to taking the drugs. It seems she worked part-time at Miss Layton's shop a while back, too. I will say that people aren't too good about where they hide their spare keys around here, Miss Layton's brother gave her a good talking to about leaving a spare key under a planter behind her shop."

"Did you get all of Whitney's jewelry back?"

"We did, but the drugs were already gone."

"Well, at least you found who was responsible." Relief flooded through Ashley that the theft hadn't been her fault. She'd done nothing wrong. Nothing at all.

"Well, I better get back to the station." Officer Moore stood looking uncomfortable and shifted from foot to foot. "I am sorry about my over-zealousness. Hope it didn't cause any trouble."

Ashley looked at the man for a moment, then held out her hand. "Apology accepted." How could she blame the man for trying to fit in?

The officer shook her hand. "Thanks, ma'am." He turned and left the clinic.

"Well, there's some more good news for you." Jerri Lynn smiled. "I'll get your charts ready. You have a busy day. And I expect it will get busier when the news gets around they caught the real thief."

* * * * *

Will left Whit's shop that evening. He'd thoroughly yelled at Whit, in a big brother way, for having a spare key in such an obvious place. All her protesting about how safe the town was did nothing to appease him. She'd finally agreed to pocket the spare key and keep it at her cottage, like any sane business owner would. He was thrilled she'd gotten her jewelry pieces back, but worried that she'd hired this Patricia Greene person in the first place. His sister was great at making jewelry, but really was clueless about running a business and possibly not the best judge of character.

Though she seemed to have Warren pegged this time. She'd been right about their father, and Will meant to keep his promise to Whit and go see Warren on his way back to Belle Island.

The new bookkeeper was in today, and she'd promised to come weekly and keep his sister on track. He'd filed the right paperwork to appease the Internal Revenue Service and filed an amended tax return for Whit. His job here was done and he could finally go back home.

He decided to swing by Sweet Caroline's and say goodbye to Caroline before he left. He entered the restaurant and Caroline waved to him. Might as well have a piece of her pecan pie, too. There was no one to tell him he'd spoil his dinner. He sat at a table by the window.

"Hi, Will. I hoped you'd stop by before you left."

"Of course." He smiled at Caroline. It had been good reconnecting with her while he'd been back in Indigo Bay.

"How about a piece of pecan pie on the house?"

"I wouldn't say no to that."

Caroline returned with the pie and sat across from him. "So, you're headed out soon?"

"Tomorrow morning."

"And what about Ashley?"

"What about her?" Will stabbed a piece of pecan pie with a little too much force.

"You two didn't work things out?"

"You could say that. She pretty much thinks I'm the last person she wants to be seen around town with."

"That's not true."

"That's what she said." He stabbed another bite of pie.

"You care about her, don't you?"

He sat for a moment, debating how to answer her. "I... do. I guess I always will. But we're different. And it seems like we bring out the worst in each other these days. Besides, she is so focused on staying here in Indigo Bay. It's her mission to make the townspeople see her as a competent doctor. She needs that."

"She *thinks* she needs that." Caroline corrected him.

"Anyway, I can't take the on again, off again thing with her. I think I wouldn't trust her even if she said she did want to give us a try. She walks away. That's what she does."

Caroline reached over and touched his hand. "Will, listen to me. You need to think good and hard about walking away from *her* this time. I've seen the way you two look at each other. I've seen the way your eyes light up when you see her. Relationships are difficult. They take work."

"I did try. I did. But she keeps insisting we're wrong for each other."

"Have you talked to her? Why she feels that way? Maybe she's just... scared. Relationships are scary. Maybe she's afraid of losing someone again, just like you are."

He looked at Caroline, always amazed at her innate ability to read people, to know what they needed.

"I think you should at least try talking to her. Tell her how you feel about her."

"If only I *knew* how I felt about her."

"Oh, you do, Will. You do. You just have to listen to your heart." Caroline got up, squeezed his shoulder, and walked away.

Will finished the pecan pie, bite by bite, thinking about everything Caroline had said. The easy thing would be to just leave tomorrow and be done with it. Put these weeks behind him.

For the first time in a long time, he wasn't sure he wanted to take the easy way out.

Chapter Seventeen

Will took a long beach walk after his talk with Caroline. Try as he might, he couldn't sort out his feelings. The evening light dimmed with the sunset, and he headed back to Whit's cottage. He cut across the beach and climbed the stairs to the deck. He looked over to see if, just by chance, Ashley might be out on her deck. But, no. The faint smell of burning wood drifted around him. Someone must be having a bonfire on the beach. He looked and saw smoke behind Ashley's cottage.

Whit came out on the deck. "What are you staring at?"

"Someone must be having a bonfire on the beach." He pointed to the smoke behind Ashley's cottage.

Or was it behind Ashley's cottage?

The hair rose on the nape of his neck. "Whit... I don't think that's on the beach. That's from Ashley's cottage. Call the fire department."

He leapt off the stairs and hit the beach running, fear

racing through him.

"Be careful. Wait for the fire department." Whit called after him.

Will rushed to the cottage, his pulse pounding in his ears. Was Ashley home? Was she okay? He took the stairs to her deck in one stride and jerked on the sliding door to the cottage.

It wouldn't budge. Locked. Maybe she wasn't home?

He pounded on it. "Ashley?" He pounded again. "Ashley are you there?"

He raced around to the front of the cottage and saw her car was there, but that didn't mean much, she usually walked around town. He tried the front door. Locked. He ran back to the sliding door and peered into the cottage. The room was filled with smoke, but through it, he could see Ashley on the floor. "Ashley!" he screamed her name.

He turned and grabbed a chair from the deck and swung it with all his might against the glass in the sliding door. It shattered around him and he lunged into the house, sinking low to his knees, mindless of the shards digging into his hands. He crawled, low, under the smoke to Ashley.

"Ashley. Are you okay?" He reached her and grabbed her with both hands.

"I…" Ashley coughed.

"Okay, don't talk. I'm getting you out of here. Hold on." He gathered her into his arms and rose unsteadily to his feet, crouching low, and raced outside into the cool, fresh, full-of-oxygen night air. He dropped to his knees and set Ashley on the sand, gasping for breath.

"Ash?"

"I'm okay." Her voice sounded thready and weak. "I fell asleep on the couch. I woke up and there was smoke. I fell and got disoriented. I heard your voice and tried to get to you."

"I found you. You're okay." His pulse pounded in his ears, his breath came out in gulps, and his eyes burned, but he paid no attention to all that. He pulled her into his lap, rocking back and forth. He could hear the sirens in the distance as he sat, holding her tucked tightly against his chest. He stroked her arms and gently swept her hair from her face.

"I thought I lost you." He whispered into her ear and drew her closer. "Don't ever scare me like that again."

Whit rushed over and dropped to the sand beside them. "Are you okay?

"Yes." Will coughed and sucked in more air.

"And Ashley?"

"I'm okay." Ashley murmured the words.

"Help is coming." Whit knelt beside him, one arm around his shoulder, peering at Ashley.

He held Ashley until the emergency medical technicians showed up. "We need to check her out. Sir? Sir? Let us exam her."

"I'm right here, Ash. I'm not going anywhere." He

whispered the words in her ear. He reluctantly released his grip on her and let the technicians do their job.

* * * * *

Ashley awoke in the hospital to find Will asleep at her bedside, his head resting on his arms on the bed. She reached over, stroked his hair, and he stirred. He lifted his head and smiled at her through sleepy, bloodshot eyes.

"Ash, you're awake. You feel okay?"

"I'm fine. You didn't need to stay all night."

"Yes, I did." He scrubbed his hands over his face. "When I saw that smoke coming from your house... I just... I thought I might lose you. I couldn't breathe. I just..."

"It's okay. I'm okay." She reached out to touch his face, streaked with soot. "You doing okay, though? There was a lot of smoke."

"I'm fine."

"The cottage?"

"There's a lot of damage. They said the fire started in the back bedroom."

"I don't use that one." Ashley frowned.

"They think it was faulty wiring. A lot of these old cottages haven't been brought all up to code. They get grandfathered in until someone remodels."

"I'm lucky you saw the smoke." Ashley clung to Will's hand. "You saved my life."

"I'm so glad I was there. One more day and I would

174

have been gone, back to Belle Island." Will took both of her hands in his. His grip was warm and strong. "Ashley, there's no way I'm leaving without telling you one thing."

"What's that?" She looked at his tired eyes, disheveled hair, and thought he'd never looked so handsome.

"I love you, Ash. I've never stopped."

Her pulse raced and the room spun. He loved her. And of course she loved him, no matter how many times she tried to convince herself that she didn't. But love alone wasn't enough, was it? Maybe when you're silly kids, but not when you're mature adults with dreams and goals.

"I love you, too, Will."

His eyes lit up.

"But... that doesn't really change things, does it?" Her heart twisted in her chest. "We want different things. We'd just make each other miserable."

His eyes clouded. "We could make it work. We're not so very different."

"Ah, my Will. We *are* so very different." They *were* different and she couldn't just leap into his arms and forget they wanted different things out of life.

"We love each other. It should be that simple." Will's face held a determined look.

"You drift through life—and I'm not saying that's wrong—for *you*. But I need structure and plans. I know that about myself. I need to know what the future holds."

"Do we ever truly know what's in our future?"

"Will, you're asking me to choose between you and my dreams. We live in different towns and you know you don't want to live in Indigo Bay."

"We'll work it out. You could come to Belle Island with me." His eyes flashed.

"Or you could come live here. You can bartend anywhere."

As soon as the words slipped out, she knew she'd hurt him. He pulled away from her.

"The same could be said about practicing medicine." He stood beside her bed and looked down at her. He slowly turned and started for the door. He paused halfway and turned to her. "We could have tried. You shouldn't be afraid to try... to give us a chance."

She saw him standing in the middle of the room, so proud, asking her to be with him. Her heart begged her to say yes, but her mind argued it would never work.

"I just... can't. It wouldn't work and then we'd have to go through all the pain again."

Will looked at her, his shoulder's set, his face a stony mask of disappointment. "I never thought of you as a quitter, Ash. But I can't make you want to try, can't make you give us a chance. I'll leave now. I'll go back home. I wish the best for you, I do. I hope those plans of yours make you very happy."

She watched him walk out the door, and the cold loneliness of the hospital room seeped into her very bones.

Chapter Eighteen

Will entered the rehab center in Savannah, Georgia. A young lady at the reception desk smiled at him. A smile like that would have garnered her an answering smile and some sweet talk just a few short weeks ago, but now he just asked to see Warren.

"He's in the sunroom now. It's just down that hallway, make a left, and you can't miss it." She smiled at him again.

He just nodded and headed down the long hallway. He entered the sunroom and found Warren sitting and working on a crossword puzzle, of course. Warren looked up, and a wide grin spread across his face. "Will. Good of you to stop in."

"It was on my way back home." Will dropped to a chair beside Warren.

"Well, it's good to see you. I hear Whit was all upset when she couldn't get ahold of me. My cell phone battery was dead and I didn't bring a charger for it. They finally found one I could use, and I called her when I got the messages. I feel horrible that she didn't find my note at first. She must have thought…" Warren's voice trailed off.

"Actually, she was pretty vocal about defending you. Saying you had changed and you wouldn't have just left without saying anything." Will screwed up his courage. "I know I didn't give you much of a chance this visit."

"You have no reason to trust me, Will, but I have changed. I hope to be able to prove that to you."

"I don't know how this is going to work…" Will was lost. He didn't know how to have a relationship with this man.

Warren reached over and put his hand over Will's. "I think we can just take it a day at a time. When are you coming back to Indigo Bay for another visit?"

"Not sure that's going to happen anytime soon." Or anytime for that matter. Unless Ashley decided to move far, far away. And *that* wasn't going to happen either.

"Well, maybe I could come with Whitney next time she goes to visit you."

"I'd like that."

Will stared at the man who he'd sworn he'd never forgive. "All I ask is that you don't hurt Whitney again."

"I won't. I promise. I can't change the past, but I can promise I'm going to be a good father to Whitney… and to you, if you let me. Or we can be whatever you'd like if you can't think of me as your father. I *am* so sorry about the past."

Will stared at Warren's hand covering his own. A hand that hadn't been there to help him as he was growing up, but one that was willing to try to build a relationship now. A tiny spot in Will's heart thawed. A part of his heart he'd kept firmly wrapped up, not daring to hope. "You know, Warren, I do forgive you for the past. Let's put it behind us. Everyone makes mistakes. You're doing a lot to make up for them. I've... missed you. I've missed the father I had before Mom died."

"I've missed you, too, son." Warren's face was flushed with gratitude and his eyes glistened.

Will cleared his throat. "Well, I should get back on the road."

"I'm glad you stopped by."

Will stood and reached out to shake his father's hand. "I'm glad I stopped by, too. I'll see you soon."

"Bye, son."

Will took a few steps across the sunroom, then turned back to Warren. "See you soon, Dad."

* * * * *

Ashley hoped a piece of Caroline's pecan pie would improve her mood. She'd been sulking around since Will left. The clinic kept her busy during the day... but the nights seemed to last forever. A loneliness like she'd never felt before settled around her. She felt all alone, which was strange since all her life she'd worked so hard to fit in and to feel like an accepted resident of Indigo Bay. She finally was getting her wish. People filled the waiting room at the clinic. Even Victoria had brought Mia in for a checkup saying something about it was too inconvenient to go into Charleston to the doctor there.

But even with all that, she still was so, so lonely.

She sat at a window by the table, watching the townsfolk walk by outside. Happy families strolled by and couples walked hand-in-hand. She saw Miss Sanderson and Maggie go into a shop across the street. Everyone seemed to have… someone.

"Did you come in for pie?" Caroline stood at the table with a welcoming smile.

"I did."

"Thought so." Caroline placed a tray with two pieces of pecan pie and a pitcher of sweet tea on the table. "Want some company?"

Ashley nodded gratefully and Caroline sat across the table from her. Caroline poured them both a tall glass of tea and doled out the pie and forks. "Pecan usually cheers a person up."

"I hope it works." Ashley took a sip of the tea.

"Want to talk about it?" Caroline leaned forward. "I'm a good listener."

"I… I just feel… wrong. Alone. Which is crazy because people in town are actually asking me to do things. I'm going to help with Ashland Belle Society's fundraiser in a few weeks. The clinic is busy. Very busy."

"You miss Will." Caroline cut right to the point.

Ashley sat back in her chair. "I do. I admit that. At one point I thought... well, it doesn't matter. He'd never stay in Indigo Bay."

"Location is all that is keeping you apart?"

"Well, that's a biggie. There's a ton of miles between us. And we're different. We want different things from life."

"Do you? Don't you think plans can sometimes change? That we sometimes need to adapt to changes? Life throws us surprises, and we need to figure out how to handle them. Life isn't all neatly planned out... and if we do plan it out, life has a way of laughing at us."

Ashley played at eating her pie. "I guess so. I did have everything planned out. I came back here to prove to everyone I was more than that geeky girl from the wrong side of town. I wanted everyone to accept me for who I am... and they do now. Don't they?" She looked at Caroline.

"Is that so important? What people think about you? I believe the only person we need to worry about pleasing is ourself. You need to believe in yourself and accept yourself... whoever you are. Whether you're the smart, geeky girl in a rundown apartment with a fabulous father who loved you very much, you know, or whether you're the town's newest doctor. What is important is if you're happy with the person you are, not what anyone else thinks about you."

Ashley set down her fork. "I... I guess I've been so busy worrying about what others thought, that I didn't stop to think about what I thought." Ashley frowned. "I am proud of me. I worked hard to become a doctor and I think I'm a darned good one."

"Exactly." Caroline smiled. "That's what's important. But you're more than just a doctor. You have to like you as a *person*."

Ashley felt her forehead crinkle. "Well, that one is tougher. I'm not sure about Ashley the person."

"What does Ashley the person want now? That's what's important."

Ashley looked at Caroline, and it was as if the kind woman's wise words had chased the fog away and she could see clearly now. She jumped up from the table. "I know exactly what I want."

* * * * *

"Whitney? You here?" Ashley called through the screen door of Whitney's cottage.

"In the kitchen, come on in."

Ashley hurried back through Whitney's cottage.

"Hey, Ashley. What's up? I was just pouring myself a glass of wine. You want one?" Whitney stood in her kitchen with a bottle of wine in one hand and a corkscrew in the other.

"No... Thanks, but... can you give me Will's address?" Ashley stood with one hand on the back of a kitchen chair.

"You going to write him?" Whitney cocked her head to one side.

"No, I'm going to go *see* him."

"I thought things were over between you? Over for good, that's what he said when he left." Whitney's voice held a protective overtone.

"I messed up. Really messed up. I was so focused on my *life plan*. Never waver, never veer off track. I thought that we wanted different things. Well, we do, I guess. But it all comes down to that fact that I love your brother."

Whitney grinned. "Of course you do. I just didn't think you were ever going to realize it."

Ashley sighed. "I thought the best thing that could happen to me was to come back and prove to the town that I'm a success, that I've made it. But even though the town has accepted me—the clinic is full every day now—I've been miserable every single minute since Will left."

"You don't say." Whitney smiled, poured herself a glass of wine, and took a sip. "I was wondering if the two of you would ever figure out that you're meant to be together."

"I don't care if all Will wants out of life is to be a bartender. If that makes him happy, I'm good with that. Great with that." Ashley walked over to the window and looked out at the sea, the waves rolling in, one after the next. "I'm fine if he wants to drift through life without a plan as long as he's happy."

"He's not exactly just a bartender." Whitney frowned.

"Didn't he tell you he owns The Lucky Duck tavern?"

Ashley turned back towards Whitney. "No, he left that part out."

"He not only owns the tavern, he owns some rental properties around town. Remember how great he was with math in school?"

Ashley nodded.

"Well, it turns out he's not only good at math, he's good at playing the market and investing."

"Really? He didn't say a word." Ashley crossed back to the kitchen table.

"He doesn't really like to talk about it. You know Will. He doesn't care what people think about him. He's pretty low key about the success he's made." Whitney's eyes shone with pride. "I'm proud of him, though. I always knew he'd do something with his life."

"But... he dropped out of high school. I thought he just wanted to float through life..." Ashley pulled out the chair and sank onto it. "I don't understand."

"He dropped out of high school to take a second job. Hasn't he ever talked to you about it? I know when we were kids we swore each other to secrecy... but didn't he talk to you? Our father disappeared that year Will turned eighteen, his senior year in high school. We were running out of money and never knew when Dad would show up. He... he was a binge drinker. He'd just disappear for weeks at a time. This time it had been a month and... well, I was worried that social workers would come and take me away."

"He never mentioned a word of this to me."

"I did make him promise. We just pretended Dad was around, or out of town on a brief business trip if anyone asked. I don't think anyone knew how often Dad was gone."

Ashley's heart plummeted. She'd judged Will so harshly all those years ago. Here he'd given up everything for his sister... and in return, Ashley had broken up with him because of what she thought was his lack of ambition. She thought back on the day they'd broken up, all those years ago. He'd tried to talk to her, asked her to listen to him, but she'd cut him off. Then he'd gotten frostily silent and his eyes had glinted with anger. He'd turned and walked away from her and hadn't said a word to her the rest of the school year. Then she'd headed to college and hadn't seen him until he showed up in Indigo Bay a few weeks ago.

Ashley sighed. "Well, now I have another problem."

"What's that?"

"Now he's going to think I only want him back because I heard he's had such success with his life."

Whitney grabbed a piece of paper and jotted down Will's address. "You need to go and talk to him and sort things out. Talk to him." Whitney handed the paper to Ashley. "But, you'll probably find him at The Lucky Duck, anyway."

"Thank you." Ashley clutched the paper. "I'm headed

out first thing in the morning."

"What about the clinic?"

"Doc Browning is back."

"I thought you wanted him to hire you on and you'd join his practice." Whitney set her glass on the table.

"I thought so, too. It was my dream, my plan. Now the only thing I want is to make things right with your brother."

"Well, he's a stubborn one." Whitney grinned. "But hopefully you can get through to him."

Ashley gave Whitney a quick hug. "Thank you. You're a great friend."

"Good luck. Make him listen to you. Tell him I said not to be pigheaded and a chump." Whitney laughed.

Ashley hurried out the door to go pack. She was going to get an early start in the morning.

Tomorrow.

Tomorrow she was going to see Will.

Chapter Nineteen

Will swiped at the countertop at The Lucky Duck. Not that it needed wiping off, but he'd tried to keep constantly busy since he'd returned. He looked up to see two regulars, Jamie and Harry, come into the tavern. They took two seats at the bar.

A group of three young women came in laughing and joking and took a table near the window.

"Go ahead." Harry tilted his head towards the women. "We'll wait."

"Nope, I'm good."

"Since when do you wait on us when some pretty ladies come into The Lucky Duck?"

"Since now. You were here first. I'll get them in a minute."

Jamie shook his head and turned to Harry. "I don't know what's wrong with him since he came back from visiting his sister."

"I don't either." Harry said in an exaggerated whisper. "It's like he's forgotten he's a lady's man."

"Knock it off." Will banged a bowl of nuts down in front of his friends.

"Just teasing. How about one of your famous basil-mo-tonic drinks." Jamie settled on the barstool. "I heard your concoction is going to become the rage all over Florida real soon now."

"I'm sure it is, just you wait and see." Will pushed all their friendly teasing aside. They were right. Just a few short weeks ago, he would have left them and hurried over to serve the women, possibly angling a date out of one of them. Now? Well, he just didn't care. One customer was just like the next.

"One famous drink, coming up. And you, Harry?"

"I have a cold draft."

"Sure thing." Will got their drinks and placed them on the bar. "You guys eating, too?"

"Nah, I'm headed back to the inn, but promised Harry a quick drink tonight."

"Well, glad you came in. I'll be back to check on you in a bit." Will walked over to the table the window and took the ladies' orders.

He served the ladies their sweet, froufrou drinks... couldn't convince them to try the basil-mo-tonic—and went back to visit with his friends.

"Who's that? It looks like she's looking for someone." Jamie tilted his head toward the door.

Will turned to see and dropped the dish cloth he was holding. He stood paralyzed, afraid he was seeing a mirage.

What was Ashley doing here at The Lucky Duck?

* * * * *

Ashley stood in the doorway of The Lucky Duck, letting her eyes adjust to the dim light after being in the bright sunshine outside. She blinked a few times and took another step inside. Her glaze swept the room, looking for Will.

She froze when she saw him standing behind the bar, not moving a muscle, like an opossum trying to hide. She wasn't having any of that. She took a deep breath and crossed the distance to the bar. "Will."

"Ashley, what are you doing here?" Will's voice was a low growl.

"I came to see you. To talk to you."

"I don't think we have anything to say." Will reached behind him and picked up a clean dishtowel from a stack on the far counter.

"We do. Please."

The two men sitting at the bar looked back and forth between Will and her. The red-headed man looked back at Will and grinned. "Don't you think you should talk to the lady?"

"Stay out of it, Jamie." Will glared at the man.

"Jamie boy is right. If the lady wants to talk, don't you think you should listen?" The other man joined in.

"Aren't you two about finished?" Will glowered at both of them.

"Nope, staying right here." The red-haired man sipped his drink and relaxed on his barstool.

"Will, can we please talk?"

"Talk away. I don't suppose I can stop you." Will grabbed a glass and started drying it. Over and over.

"Fine. I'll talk here." Whitney had been right. Her brother *was* stubborn. "I'm sorry, Will. I am. I apologize. I know there's no reason in the world you should believe me this time, but I came to ask you to give me another chance. I want us to try again."

Will put down the glass.

"Please. I made a mistake sending you away. I've been so miserable. I've missed you so much. All that time chasing my dream of being the big doctor in town and everyone accepting me… well, none of that made me happy. *You* make me happy."

The red-haired man stood and dropped some bills on the bar. "Um, come on Harry. I think we're finished, aren't we? Let's leave these two to sort things out."

The other man took one last swig of his beer and slid off his barstool. "Listen to the woman, Willie. You've been a cranky old geezer since you came back from your trip. Should have known it was woman troubles." He turned to her and nodded his head. "Ma'am."

"He's a stubborn one, but make him listen to you." The red-haired man tossed over his shoulder as the two men walked away.

She slid onto a vacated barstool. "Will, I love you. I want to be with you."

Will still looked doubtful.

"I told Whitney I didn't care if you wanted to be a bartender your whole life if it made you happy. I've learned that doing what makes you happy is what is important. Not following a plan, not worrying about what people think of you." She paused. "And I decided I wanted to be with you before Whitney told me you owned this tavern and some other places around town… so don't think I'm being superficial and I'm here now because I know how much you've done with your life."

Will came around the bar and sat on the barstool next to her, still not saying a word.

"Will… can you please forgive me? I promise I won't waver again. I can't imagine my life without you in it."

Will's eyes sparkled. "Really?"

"Really." She reached out and took his hands in hers.

"I can't imagine my life without you, either. These last days since I left Indigo Bay… they've been the loneliest days of my life. You… you complete me and make me whole, Ash. You always have. Ever since we became friends as kids. You just… get me."

"I can't believe you didn't set me straight all those years ago on why you dropped out of high school."

"You know?" Will's forehead wrinkled.

"Whitney told me. You should have told me back

then. I was so self-righteous with all my big plans. But Whit said it was your secret with her and no one else knew. I get that. I just… I'm just so embarrassed at how I treated you then."

"It's okay." Will's voice was low.

She squeezed his hands. "So do you think we can try again?"

Will leaned over and pressed a kiss to her lips. A thrill of joy raced through her as she kissed him back. He stood and pulled her from her seat, wrapping his arms around her. "I think there is nothing I'd rather do than spend my entire life working things out with you. It might take a long time. Years and years."

"Yes, we should try for a very long time." She whispered against his neck.

"We should try forever." Will whispered back.

* * * * *

The next morning Will stood at Lighthouse Point with Ashley by his side, watching the sunrise. "The sun rises in the east, over the bay here at Belle Island, but the reflections in the clouds over the ocean are pretty great. We throw a mean sunset here, too."

"I think this is the most beautiful sunrise I've ever spent with you."

Will smiled and pulled her closer. "You know, we have a town legend about Lighthouse Point here on the island."

"What's that?" Ashley snuggled up next to him.

"If you make a wish at Lighthouse Point and throw a shell into the ocean, your wish will come true."

Ashley turned her face up to his and smiled. She pulled away, leaned down, and picked up a shell with her slender fingers. The morning light lit up her face and she turned a brilliant smile to him. "Let's make wishes."

He reached down and picked up a perfect shell near his feet.

He watched while she closed her eyes for a moment then opened them. She turned and threw her shell out into the waves. He closed his own eyes, then opened them and tossed his shell after hers.

"What was your wish?" Ashley looked at him.

"My wish?"

"Yes, tell me." Ashley eyes shone with happiness, a good look on her.

"I…" He took a deep breath and dropped to one knee. "I wished that you'd marry me."

Ashley's face broke into a smile, her eyes glistened with tears. "I wished that we'd get married."

"So that's a yes? You'll marry me?"

"That's a yes." She dropped to her knees beside him on the sand and leaned against him. He wrapped his arms around her while the sunrise exploded into brilliant colors around them.

DEDICATION AND ACKNOWLEDGMENTS

This book is dedicated to all the lovers of glorious sunrises.

*****

Cover by Najla Qamber Designs

www.najlaqamberdesigns.com

ABOUT THE AUTHOR

Kay Correll writes stories that are a cross between contemporary romance and women's fiction. She likes her books with a healthy dose of happily ever after. Her stories are set in the fictional small towns of Comfort Crossing, Mississippi and Belle Island, Florida. While her books are a series, each one can be read as a stand-alone story.

Kay lives in the Midwest of the U.S. and can often be found out and about with her camera, taking a myriad of photographs which she likes to incorporate into her book covers. When not lost in her writing or photography, she can be found spending time with her ever-supportive husband, knitting, working in her garden, or playing with her puppies—two cavaliers and one naughty but adorable Australian shepherd. Kay and her husband also love to travel. When it comes to vacation time, she is torn between a nice trip to the beach or the mountains—but the mountains only get considered in the summer—she swears she's allergic to snow.

Made in the USA
Las Vegas, NV
13 March 2024

87175304R00121